FiELD OF SCREAMS

FIELD OF SCREAMS

Wendy Parris

DELACORTE PRESS

Text copyright © 2023 by Wendy Parris
Jacket art copyright © 2023 by Simon Prades

All rights reserved. Published in the United States by Delacorte Press,
an imprint of Random House Children's Books,
a division of Penguin Random House LLC, New York.

Delacorte Press is a registered trademark and the colophon
is a trademark of Penguin Random House LLC.

Visit us on the Web! rhcbooks.com

Educators and librarians, for a variety of teaching tools,
visit us at RHTeachersLibrarians.com

Library of Congress Cataloging-in-Publication Data is available upon request.
ISBN 978-0-593-57000-5 (trade pbk.) — ISBN 978-0-593-56998-6 (lib. bdg.) —
ISBN 978-0-593-56999-3 (ebook)

The text of this book is set in 12-point Adobe Jenson Pro.
Interior design by Jen Valero

Printed in the United States of America
10 9 8 7 6 5 4 3 2 1
First Edition

To my Iowa grandmothers,
Glenys Jean
and
Mary Kathryn

ONE

Rebecca fought to keep her eyes open as she peered across the living room into the dim kitchen. The glowing numbers on the microwave clock read 12:00. Midnight. She sighed and sank deeper into the couch. The way she figured it, the later she stayed awake, the slower time would move—and the longer it would feel until she had to leave home. She dug a handful of hot popcorn from the bowl in her lap and crammed it into her mouth.

On the TV screen a young girl crept through a dark graveyard full of crumbling tombstones. A ghostly figure followed her, reaching out a bony hand. Creepy organ music surged.

"*Run!*" Rebecca whispered.

Two sharp taps exploded in the quiet behind her. Rebecca jerked in surprise, making popcorn fly from the bowl. She hit the mute button on the remote, her heart pounding. Silence. Her eyes swept the small, cluttered room and the entryway piled with suitcases. Nothing moved. No sound came from Mom's room above.

Okay. Her ears must be playing tricks on her. She turned back to the TV.

The tapping came again, this time in a staccato rhythm Rebecca had heard a kazillion times. She dropped the remote, leapt to her feet, and raced to the front door. Through the peephole she spied a shadowy figure hovering on the stoop, a silhouette of braids cascading from under a ball cap. She cracked open the door.

"You scared the heck outta me," she hissed.

"Ha!" Rebecca's best friend, Jenna, grabbed her arm and pulled her outside into the sticky summer night. "Gotcha."

"Shhhh!" Rebecca closed the door behind her. "My mom doesn't know I'm up."

"Please. She'd sleep through a tornado." Jenna pushed a silver gift bag into Rebecca's hands. "I totally forgot to give this to you before."

A warm glow spread through Rebecca's chest. "What is it?"

"Something for your car trip tomorrow. In case you

get bored with your mom and her eighties music." Even in the faint light, Jenna's brown eyes sparkled with mischief.

Rebecca's warm glow sputtered and died. "Don't remind me."

She was leaving the next day to spend the rest of the summer babysitting her two-year-old cousin at an Iowa farmhouse. Meanwhile, Jenna would be riding horses, water-skiing, and basically having a blast at Camp Birchdale. It wasn't fair.

"Come on, it won't be that bad," Jenna said. "Your aunt and uncle sound cool."

"How would I know?" Rebecca muttered. "It's not like they've bothered with me in forever."

Jenna planted her hands on her hips. "You promised you'd give them a chance."

"Yeah, yeah." Rebecca picked at her thumbnail. Hanging out with Uncle Jon, Aunt Sylvie, and their little boy, Justin, was nice in theory, but in reality it was too little, too late. This reunion, or whatever it was, should have happened when she was young and begging to see Dad's side of the family. Now she was older and had things to do. Like go to Cubs games in the city or ride her bike to the beach.

Or go to camp with her best friend.

"You don't fool me." Jenna gave her a no-nonsense look. "I know you're curious about them. Now open your present."

"Yes, ma'am." Rebecca dug into the bag and pulled out a heavy paperback book. On the cover was a black-and-white sketch of a dead tree looming over a misty cornfield. She tipped the book toward the streetlight and read the title: *Heart-Stopping Heartland Hauntings*. The letters shimmered and dripped with red bloodlike splatters. A delicious shiver crawled up her spine. "Awesome."

"Look on the bright side," Jenna said. "You've always wanted to see a ghost. An old farmhouse in the middle of nowhere is the perfect place."

"I guess." Rebecca mulled this over. She hadn't really thought of it that way. Jenna was always so much more positive than she was.

The rumble of a loose tailpipe erupted, and a black car cruised along the street. Both girls shrank back, plastering themselves into the shadows. The car turned at the end of the block and headed to the alley behind the houses. Jenna's brother was home from his job delivering pizzas.

"Go, before you get in trouble." Rebecca threw her arms around Jenna. "I'm going to miss you so much."

"I wish you were coming with me." Jenna's voice was

muffled against Rebecca's shoulder. "I can't believe the next time we see each other, we'll be in junior high."

Rebecca's throat tightened, cutting off the *goodbye* she wanted to say. Jenna pulled away and hopped down the stairs, braids flying. Rebecca watched through tears as her friend disappeared into the small brick bungalow next door. The upcoming six weeks were going to be the worst. She and Jenna hadn't been apart for more than eight days since kindergarten.

"What are you doing?"

Rebecca whirled around. Mom stood in the doorway wrapped in a white bathrobe, her blond hair in a messy ponytail, eyes sleepy behind crooked glasses.

"Nothing," Rebecca said. "Jenna dropped off a present for me."

She pulled the book to her chest, but it was too late. Mom had already scanned the title.

"Seriously? Jenna of all people should know better." Mom crossed her arms. "I thought you were over this ghost obsession. We do not need a repeat of last summer's fiasco."

Rebecca lifted her chin. "How were we supposed to know Mrs. Alvarado's son was in town? And why would he walk around an empty house with a flashlight in the middle of the night?"

"Why would you try to break into a house to prove it was haunted?" Mom shot back. She lifted a shaky hand and smoothed a flyaway wisp of hair from her eyes. "I was absolutely terrified to get a call from the police at two a.m. You girls are lucky you didn't get arrested. Or hurt."

"But it was totally spooky the way the light flickered and the footsteps—"

"There are no such things as ghosts," Mom said through clenched teeth.

How do you know? Rebecca wanted to yell. She bit her tongue instead. Lately, she and Mom had been arguing more than usual. Jenna said fighting with your parents was a normal part of growing up, but it made Rebecca queasy. She and Mom had been the perfect team the past six years, just the two of them, together. But lately it seemed they were always on opposite sides.

Rebecca ran her fingers over the raised letters on the book's cover. "This is only for fun. But I guess you don't want me to have any of that."

Mom clicked her tongue. "Honey, that's not true." She peered over the top of her glasses at Rebecca. "Have you been crying?"

"Not really." Rebecca ducked her head, letting her hair fall in a brown, curly curtain around her face.

"Oh, Co-Cap." Co-Cap was Mom's nickname for her, short for *co-captain*. She put her arm around Rebecca's shoulder and guided her into the house. "I'm sorry you're not going with Jenna this summer. We just can't afford—"

"I know." Rebecca sniffed, squirming with guilt. Mom always worried about money. "It's fine."

"I promise, when I get my raise next year, I'll send you to camp, okay?"

Rebecca nodded. When Mom got her PhD, she would make more money as a high school English teacher, money they could really use. Summer break was her time to finish her dissertation. So when Jon and Sylvie had invited them to Iowa, offering her a quiet place to focus on writing, Mom had been thrilled. Then they'd agreed to pay Rebecca to watch little Justin while they worked and got ready for their new baby. All that, plus the chance to get to know each other better and—*bam!*—the decision had been made. Mom called it a "win-win." Rebecca wasn't so sure.

"We'll make this summer as fun as possible for you," Mom continued. "We'll go to county fairs and take bike rides and your uncle Jon scouted out a local pool not far away. It won't be all babysitting, okay?"

"I guess." Rebecca forced a weak smile.

"All right, turn off the TV and go to bed please." Mom planted a kiss on Rebecca's cheek. "We need to wake up early."

"Okay." Rebecca didn't fight her. She'd watched the scary movie before and knew how it ended. Plus, she had *Heart-Stopping Heartland Hauntings* to keep her awake and her mind off the next day.

Upstairs in her room, Rebecca flipped a switch, turning on the dozens of twinkling lights strung across the ceiling. She swept a mass of colorful pillows from the bed, climbed between the sheets, and opened her new book. The table of contents listed fantastically eerie titles like "Beware the Banshee of Beloit" and "What Lurks in Devil's Backbone Park?" She snuggled in and flipped to chapter one, "The Phantom of Full Moon Lake." The first sentence stopped her cold.

Young, open-minded believers are the people most likely to encounter a ghost.

She bit her lip. That described her to the core. So why hadn't she seen one yet?

"Lights off, please," Mom called from across the hall.

Rebecca snapped shut the book and tossed it on the pillow next to her. Fine. She'd read on the car trip. Reaching to turn off the lights, her hand bumped the small oval picture frame that sat on her nightstand. She picked it up.

The picture inside showed Dad holding her when she was six years old, a week before he'd passed away. Their cheeks were pressed together, their eyes the exact same round shape and hazel color with thick lashes. Rebecca had given up ever meeting his ghost—he would have shown himself by now if he was ever going to. Plus, she'd done the research. Ghosts were spirits of people who had died violently or were out for revenge. Dad had passed peacefully and surrounded by family, from a heart condition he'd had his whole life. Nothing unexpected.

Rebecca set the picture on top of *Heart-Stopping Heartland Hauntings,* so she'd remember to take it to Iowa, and switched off the lights. Jenna could be right. A farmhouse over a hundred years old could be the perfect spot for a ghost. If she got lucky, this summer might actually be exciting.

Maybe she'd find her own "heart-stopping haunting."

TWO

Rebecca jerked awake. Outside the car window, an endless blur of green cornfields whizzed by under a hazy sun. She peeled her sweaty legs away from the hot seat. Mom sat next to her, tapping the steering wheel and humming along with the radio.

"Welcome back, Sleeping Beauty," Mom said.

"How long was I out?" Rebecca croaked, her throat parched. She rolled down her window to get some fresh air.

"So long that we're almost there," Mom said.

Rebecca blinked, the fog of sleep lifting. This visit was really happening. A twinge of nerves hit her. The last time she'd seen Uncle Jon and Aunt Sylvie was years ago at Dad's funeral. Until January, they'd lived far away in Seattle and called her only on Christmas or her birthday. Then Uncle Jon inherited the old Graff family farmhouse and moved to Iowa, only a half-day drive from Chicago. And now they were supposed to act like one big happy family. She straightened anxiously in her seat.

The car slowed and turned from the country road onto a long gravel driveway lined with lacy white wildflowers. Ahead on a gentle rise stood a two-story yellow farmhouse, a weathered barn towering behind. Planters bursting with blossoms decorated a wraparound porch. The scene looked like a movie set—way too cozy to be haunted. Rebecca's shoulders drooped.

"Well, they've fixed up the outside, at least," Mom said, pulling up near the front porch. She switched off the ignition.

Instantly, the world went quiet—quieter than Rebecca had ever known it could be. She gazed through her open window at the house. A lot of lives had passed through this place. This was where the Graff family had lived for generations, where her dad and Uncle Jon spent summers as kids visiting their Grandpa Sam. She kinda remembered Dad telling her bedtime stories about fishing in a creek and jumping into huge piles of hay from the loft in the barn. Mom said he'd loved visiting Iowa.

Now that she was actually at the farm, Rebecca's curiosity stirred. She'd been so focused on missing camp with

Jenna, she hadn't realized it might be interesting to find out what Dad's life had been like when he was a kid.

A sun catcher hanging in an upstairs window glinted in the light, flashing directly into her face. She closed her eyes for a second, and when she opened them again, the flash was gone.

The bright blue front door burst open. Uncle Jon, tall and athletic with a scruffy brown beard, leapt down the porch steps. "Christine, you're early!"

Mom climbed out of the car beaming. "Traffic was no problem. Great to see you, Jon."

Rebecca's stomach fluttered as she watched them hug. She wasn't sure how to act. Stalling for time, she leaned down and scooped *Heart-Stopping Heartland Hauntings* from the floor, and stuffed it into her backpack. She sighed. So much for having something to do during the trip. She'd been too carsick to read.

"Car! Vroom!" yelled a high-pitched voice.

A small white-blond boy careened around the corner of the house followed by a pregnant woman in a billowing blue maternity dress. Cousin Justin and Aunt Sylvie. Justin spotted Rebecca in the car and stopped dead, popping his thumb into his mouth. As Aunt Sylvie reached his side, he buried his face into her leg, suddenly shy.

"I feel you, buddy," Rebecca whispered.

"Welcome," called Aunt Sylvie. Her cheeks were flushed and her light-brown hair piled in a messy bun. She wasn't due for another month, but her baby bump was so big, it looked to Rebecca like she could give birth at any second.

"Becks, get out here!" Uncle Jon loped around to the passenger side of the car. As Rebecca emerged, he shook his head. "Man. The older you get, the more I see Ben in you."

Rebecca almost dropped her backpack in surprise. She was used to seeing Uncle Jon in Christmas card photos, not face-to-face. Standing in front of him was like looking into a mirror. He had the Graff family eyes, exactly like hers. Exactly like Dad's. "You look like him, too," she blurted.

Uncle Jon smiled. "I've heard that before."

No one said anything for a moment, like they all were thinking about Dad. The sun dipped behind a cloud, almost as if it shared their sadness. Rebecca fidgeted and edged toward the porch. "Um, can I use the bathroom?"

"Oh, honey, of course," said Aunt Sylvie. "Right this way."

Justin grabbed his mom's hand and pointed at the car. "Mommy! Car!"

"Hold on, sweetie, let me show—"

"Mommy!" He struggled to pull Aunt Sylvie to the car. "Now!"

"It's okay," Rebecca said. "I can find it on my own. Cars are cool, huh, Justin?" She shouldered her backpack and winked at him as she maneuvered around Aunt Sylvie.

"We'll be in soon," called Uncle Jon.

Rebecca had already escaped up the steps, through the front door and into the house. The sharp smell of fresh paint immediately attacked her nose. She paused a moment, taking it all in. In spite of the sparkling-white walls in the entryway, the place had definitely seen better days. The wood floor under her feet was scratched, dull, and dented. To her right was a living room loaded with outdated furniture and a sleek purple couch, probably a mix of Graff family leftovers and Jon and Sylvie's stuff. Down a hall and through an archway ahead was a kitchen with old-fashioned metal cabinets. Everything seemed homey enough.

A staircase with a crooked banister hugged the wall to her left. Rebecca beelined toward it, anxious to find the room that would be hers for the rest of the summer. As she climbed the steps, they creaked under her feet, exactly like they should in an old house. Her spirits rose.

The exterior might look too cheerful for a ghost, but the inside had the right atmosphere.

On the second floor, a long hallway ran from the back of the house to the front. Some doors stood open. Justin's room, overflowing with toys, was easy to pick out. So was her aunt and uncle's room with its big bed, and the small nursery with the waiting crib. Three doors along the middle of the hall were closed and Rebecca tried them all—the first was locked, the second led to a linen closet, the third to a bathroom. That left two small bedrooms at the front of the house. She entered one.

It was almost like she'd whooshed back in time a hundred years. A blue rag rug covered the floor, a carved antique rocking chair was nestled in one corner, and a white iron bed faced the door. On the nightstand, a clock with hands and a face instead of digital numbers rested atop a yellowed square of lace. The space was neat and simple, the polar opposite of her messy room at home. Rebecca liked it anyway. If she got to pick, she'd choose this room for sure.

Muffled voices came from outside. She walked to the front window and parted the white lace curtains. There hung a round crystal sun catcher, the one that had flashed at her before. Below, Justin ran in circles around the yard while the adults huddled together in deep discussion. Suddenly Aunt Sylvie glanced up at the window. Rebecca ducked out of sight. Somehow she could tell they were talking about her.

She pulled her new cell phone, really her mom's old one, from her back pocket. It showed only one signal bar. Great. Not that Jenna was allowed to text or email from camp, but still. Rebecca's real life seemed far away, totally unreachable.

A creak reverberated from somewhere deep in the house. "I'm up here," Rebecca called. Tucking her phone in her pocket, she peered out the doorway. From her spot at the end of the bed she could see straight down the length of the hall. No one was in sight.

She ventured to the side window. Outside was a vast cornfield, a dark-green ocean of plants spreading as far as a dozen baseball fields toward the horizon. Beyond it sprawled another farm, alive with action—a tiny tractor chugged into a hulking red barn, small figures roved near a tall silo, and a black pickup cruised the driveway trailing a wake of dust. Directly below her a plot of grass stretched to the left and merged with the backyard, where a gnarled maple tree cast a twisted shadow.

But it was the cornfield that snagged Rebecca's attention. The sheer size of it was overwhelming. Not a leaf stirred in its depths. She imagined being trapped in the middle of it, not knowing the quickest way out, following one of its rows for what seemed like forever, hidden things grabbing at her—

A screen door banged downstairs, rescuing Rebecca from her thoughts.

"Honey, where are you?" Mom called. "Did you find your room?" Footsteps thumped on the stairs.

"I hope so," Rebecca said, moving to the doorway.

Mom marched along the hall, lugging her suitcase. The linen closet door was open a crack, and she pushed it closed as she walked by. "Good. Jon pointed out this one for me." She swept into the room beside Rebecca's.

Out of nowhere, a dark streak shot across the floor past Rebecca's feet. She jumped, bashing into the rocking chair as a furry black tail vanished under the bed.

"Co-Cap?" Mom called.

The blue gingham dust ruffle hanging from the bed frame quivered. Rebecca tiptoed closer and fell to her knees. She gingerly lifted the cloth.

One green eye glowed at her. Where the other eye should have been was a jagged pink seam.

Rebecca screeched. She scrambled to her feet, then backed up to the doorway and right into her mom.

"What's going on?" Mom asked.

"Something's under my bed." Rebecca braced her palm against the wall to steady herself. "But it only has one eye."

A low meow came from behind the dust ruffle.

"Oh, that must be Jade." Mom waved her hand like it was no big deal. "Jon mentioned that a couple of farm cats hang around outside. She's the one who sneaks into the house from time to time. She's tame. Don't worry."

"I'm not worried," Rebecca sputtered. "She just scared the heck out of me."

"I thought you liked being scared," Mom teased.

"Not by a freaky one-eyed cat!" Rebecca's heart was still racing. She was not in the mood to be made fun of.

"You're right," Mom said. She gently pushed a stray curl from Rebecca's forehead. "Sorry."

Rebecca tossed her head, making the curl flop back over her eyes. She'd asked Mom over and over not to touch her hair. "What happened to her eye?"

"They think she got into a fight with a raccoon or something. Here, kitty." Mom bent toward the bed and clicked her tongue. Jade stayed hidden. Mom slapped her hands on her thighs and straightened. "If she doesn't come out on her own, I'm sure Jon can get her." She walked out the door.

Rebecca eyed the dust ruffle. The second Mom crossed

into her own room, Jade scampered out from under the bed and trotted into the hall. The linen closet door gaped wide open. The cat slithered inside.

"If your closet isn't big enough, you can put some things in mine," Mom called.

"Hold on." Rebecca froze, fixated on the linen closet. "Didn't you close that door?"

"What door?" The zing of a suitcase zipper opening rang out. Mom was already unpacking.

"The linen closet's, the door in the middle of the hall." From her room, Rebecca could just make out Jade crouching in the shadows under the lowest shelf, her tail flicking back and forth.

"I don't know," Mom said. "Maybe?"

"You totally shut it. I heard it click." Rebecca kept her eyes on Jade. "But now it's wide open. I mean, not just a crack but wide—"

"Well, old houses are quirky, what can I say?" A drawer thumped open in Mom's room. "Please don't start with your overactive imagination. What, do you think a ghost opened the door?"

"I didn't say that." A flicker of irritation ran through Rebecca.

"I need you on your best behavior, all right? None of the ghost stuff. Please."

"Fine." Rebecca plopped on the bed and kicked off her flip-flops. Mom could be so annoying. The door had opened by itself. That was a fact, not her imagination. If Jenna were here, she'd believe her. She gloomily pictured her best friend swimming in Lake Birchdale, laughing and having fun with her cabinmates.

In the hall, Jade inched out of the linen closet and toward the top of the stairs. As she passed the locked door, she halted and turned her head slowly to face it. A long hiss seeped from her mouth. The hair on Rebecca's arms rose.

Suddenly the hiss cut out. Jade rocketed down the stairs and out of sight.

Hmmmm. Now, that was interesting. Rebecca wondered what was behind that locked door.

THREE

The Graff household was loud and busy, something Rebecca wasn't used to at all. The only other relatives she'd visited were Mom's parents in Florida, and they mostly read books and went to bed early. Between Uncle Jon's booming voice, Justin's cute but nonstop talking, and Aunt Sylvie's questions about what "tweens are into these days," Rebecca's brain was overloaded by dinnertime. Luckily once the dishes were done everyone disappeared upstairs—Mom to finish unpacking, Uncle Jon and Aunt Sylvie to supervise Justin's bath. Rebecca grabbed the chance to be alone and explore.

As she opened the back door, a wall of sticky air smacked her in the face. Rebecca plowed forward onto the deck and shut the door behind her, trapping Uncle Jon's newly installed air-conditioning inside. She could actually feel the frizz springing from her head. She pulled an elastic band from her wrist and swooshed her hair off her neck and into a ponytail. Much better.

Clouds piled in the sky, blocking out the sunset, but sparks from lightning bugs dotted the twilight. Rebecca stepped into the scrubby grass, her flip-flops slapping against her heels. She passed a couple of picnic tables, an inflated baby pool, and a traffic jam of toy trucks on her way to the barn.

In the spring, when Mom had learned the barn had a small storage room, she'd asked Uncle Jon if she could use it as an office, out of everyone's way. "Then I won't be tempted to talk to anyone and I can concentrate," she'd said, her face set with determination. She'd spent her first hours at the farm cleaning the storage room, while Rebecca had played games with Justin. A dusty old barn seemed like a strange place to write. Rebecca wanted to check it out.

As she entered through a side door, her eyes widened. The only barn she'd ever been inside was the quaint, brightly lit demonstration barn at Chicago's Lincoln Park Zoo. This dim, massive space was way different. The roof arched three stories above her into darkness, birds flapping and cooing in the rafters. Ladders, bikes, garden hoses, and a riding lawn mower littered the cracked concrete floor. Straight ahead, empty stalls lined the far wall. Above them jutted a large wooden platform, probably the loft Dad and Uncle Jon had jumped from long ago.

A door stood half open in a corner. Rebecca crossed to it, reached inside, and felt around the wall until she found a switch. A harsh fluorescent light buzzed on, revealing a small wood-paneled room. Tall bookcases jam-packed with paper files and *Farmers' Almanac*s teetered against one wall. An air conditioner stuck out of the single window. Mom's laptop rested on a rickety aluminum desk.

Rebecca shook her head. What a dingy space. Mom could be so weird. The house Wi-Fi probably barely reached the barn. She switched off the light and turned back to face the main room.

For a second she pictured the barn long ago, full of life. Horses and cows munching hay in the stalls, a big tractor rumbling through wide-open doors, chickens scratching in the sawdust. Two little boys whooping and leaping from the loft into piles of hay, their laughter floating into the rafters.

Out of the corner of her eye, she glimpsed a white shape flit noiselessly across the floor. Rebecca turned to look but whatever it was—maybe another cat?—seemed to have vanished behind a plastic storage bin. The birds had gone quiet. She crept over, her shoes making a soft shuffling sound, and peeked behind the bin.

There was nothing there but dirty cement.

An uneasy chill settled over her. The shadows in the corners lengthened. There was no soft hay to land in anymore. The barn was only a desolate shell that held junk people wanted to hide. Suddenly Rebecca needed to get out of there. She fled to the door and didn't stop running until she was in the middle of the backyard.

As she caught her breath, Rebecca focused on the warm, welcoming light spilling from the windows of the house. Everything was fine. She wasn't used to how different things were in the country, that was all.

Cornfields surrounded the yard on three sides. Uncle Jon had said that farmers wanted corn to grow "thigh high by the Fourth of July." Well, the Fourth had just passed and these plants were more like chin high, to Rebecca at least. A wooden swing hung from the maple tree she'd noticed from her window. She wandered over to it and eased onto the seat, testing if it would hold her weight. It did. She pushed off from the ground and began to pump her legs.

The lightning bugs had settled in the fields, hundreds of tiny sparks flickering among the stalks. Rebecca watched, mesmerized. In her neighborhood there'd only ever be ten lightning bugs, tops, floating around at a time. Her eyes landed on the back corner of the yard, where two fields met and a narrow path ran into the corn. The path beckoned, daring her to find where it led. She slid off the swing.

When she reached the edge of the yard, Rebecca saw the path traveled in a straight line away from the back of the farmhouse. In the deepening darkness, she couldn't tell where it ended. She knew the farm with a silo was beyond the side field but had no clue what was past this one.

There was a crackle down the path. A stalk shook violently and went still. She sensed someone or something crouching low, hiding in the dense rows. Her pulse jumped.

"Hello?" Her voice fell flat, deadened by the corn. Humidity flowed at her in invisible waves and drenched her skin. If she was quiet maybe whatever it was would come out. She waited, holding her breath.

"Hey, Becks!"

Rebecca whirled around, swiping her elbow on a sharp-edged leaf. Uncle Jon waved from the deck, his white T-shirt glowing in the dusk.

"Come inside before the mosquitos eat you alive," he called. "I've got a surprise for you."

A thin line of blood trailed across Rebecca's skin where the corn had scratched her. "Be right there," she answered.

As Uncle Jon went inside, she faced the path again, but the spell had been broken. Whoever or whatever had been there was definitely gone. Rebecca swatted a mosquito away from her ear. Nobody in their right mind would be skulking around a sticky, suffocating cornfield when it was getting dark. It'd probably been a deer. Mom could be right—she had an overactive imagination. Not that Rebecca would ever in a million, trillion years admit it out loud.

As she trekked to the farmhouse, the back of her neck prickled, like she was being watched. It took all of her nerve not to break into a run.

An icy blast of air-conditioning welcomed her inside. Upstairs, Mom was taking a shower and Aunt Sylvie sang lullabies to Justin. In the hall, the linen closet door was ajar. Rebecca pushed it shut as she passed, silently daring it to open. It didn't.

Uncle Jon entered the hall carrying a large cardboard box. "Did you check out your mom's office, Becks?"

Rebecca flinched. Where had this "Becks" nickname come from? Nobody ever called her that. "Uh, yeah."

"I mean, is she quirky or what? Who wants to hang

out in an old barn?" He breezed past her and went into her room.

Rebecca trailed behind, brooding. It was okay for her to complain about Mom's quirks, but other people shouldn't. Especially people who barely knew either of them.

"You know, your dad stayed in this room when we were little," Uncle Jon said, pausing near the rocking chair. "He loved it. At home we had to share a room."

"Really?" This was news to Rebecca. She wondered if it would be fun or annoying to split your private space with someone else. Probably a little bit of both.

"We were such city kids, living in Chicago, this place was like heaven to us." Uncle Jon scanned the room with a faraway expression. "My Grandpa Sam was the last real Graff family farmer. My dad wanted nothing to do with corn."

"Why?" Rebecca asked.

"The grass is always greener, right? He'd grown up here and wanted more excitement, so he headed to Chicago the first chance he got. But he and Mom made sure Ben and I got to experience country life every summer. I'm grateful for that." He grinned, his teeth white in contrast to his dark beard. "Anyway, may I sit?"

"Okay," Rebecca said. She eyed the box curiously. They settled on the edge of the bed.

"I found this in the attic when we moved in," Uncle Jon said. He tipped the box so Rebecca could read the words written across the top.

BEN'S—KEEP OUT

Her eyes widened. "This was my dad's?"

"Yup." The trace of a smile played across Uncle Jon's face. "Grandpa Sam let us each keep some stuff here, so we didn't have to take things back and forth when we visited."

He pushed the box across the patchwork quilt toward her. Rebecca had seen samples of her dad's adult handwriting, so she could tell he'd written on this box— his *B* in *Ben* was big and bold—but she'd never seen his younger scrawl.

"How come it's still here?" she asked.

Uncle Jon rubbed a palm across his scruffy chin. "Well, Grandpa Sam died the fall I was nine and Ben was twelve. We never came here again after Great-Uncle Carl took over."

"You didn't?"

"No. Carl was a loner. He sold the rest of the farmland and basically holed up in the house. The guy never threw anything away, though. The attic is so stuffed, I never would've found this box if it wasn't right at the top of the stairs." He pointed down the hall. "See that closed door? That goes to the attic. We keep it locked so Justin can't get up there and get hurt. That place is a hazard."

"Got it," Rebecca said. So, Jade had hissed at the attic door.

Uncle Jon nodded. "Go ahead. Open the box."

Hesitantly, Rebecca parted the cardboard flaps. Inside was a jumble of stuff: a stack of old comic books, a boomerang, a tackle box, a couple of sci-fi paperbacks.

"That comic book collection is probably worth a lot," Uncle Jon said. "It's yours now. Maybe it will pay for college."

Rebecca reached into the box and ruffled through the stack. A bunch of old superhero comics. She wasn't really a fan, but still. Her dad had touched these things and kept each of them for a reason. They'd been important to him.

"Whatcha reading?" Uncle Jon leaned across her and took *Heart-Stopping Heartland Hauntings* from the nightstand. He examined the cover. "Well, well, well."

Rebecca's guard went up. She couldn't tell if he thought the book was a joke, like Mom did, or if he was actually interested. "What do you mean?"

"The apple doesn't fall far from the tree," Uncle Jon

said. "Your dad was obsessed with supernatural stuff when he was young."

"He was?" A tiny zap, like a jolt of electricity, sparked in Rebecca's chest.

"Oh, yeah." Uncle Jon's eyes crinkled with affection, to her relief. "Ben was way into Bigfoot and aliens and ghosts—all of that stuff. He even wrote away to some paranormal society for information once. No internet in the old days, you know."

"Wait." The tiny zap ignited into a full-on charge and raced through Rebecca's body. "My dad believed in ghosts?"

"Absolutely. Grandpa Sam used to say Ben had an overactive imagination."

"What?" Rebecca bit back a giggle. Her dad was told that, too? She leaned forward eagerly. "Did he ever see a ghost?"

"Of course he didn't." Uncle Jon laughed. "I mean, that stuff might be fun to read about, but don't believe a word of it."

Rebecca pressed her lips together. Great, another doubter like Mom. "Why not?"

"There's always a simple explanation for any so-called proof people give that ghosts exist." Uncle Jon put his hand over hers. "This house might be old and creaky, but I've never, ever experienced anything remotely spooky here. Neither did my grandparents. Believe me, Ben asked them. You don't need to worry about ghosts."

"I'm not worried." Rebecca pulled her hand away. She didn't feel like arguing.

Uncle Jon's expression grew serious. "Do you think you should read that book before bed? Your mom mentioned you used to have terrible dreams—"

"What?" Rebecca stiffened. Mom had talked about that—about her—behind her back? "That was when I was a little kid. I don't have them anymore."

"Okay, I'm sorry. I'm only trying to look out for you." Uncle Jon rested his hands on his knees. "Becks, I know Sylvie and I haven't been around much for you over the years. We lived so far away, and my job . . . Well, it's complicated."

"It's okay." Rebecca studied a polka-dotted square on the quilt. Adults always said their jobs were complicated.

"Point is, we're here now," Uncle Jon said. "And we want to be more like family, going forward. Justin adores you already. We're happy you're here."

"Thanks." Rebecca shifted on the bed. This was awkward. She wasn't going to lie to him and say she was thrilled to be in Iowa, but it was nice he was trying.

Uncle Jon cleared his throat. "We've decided to have a barbecue tomorrow night, so you can meet some of the people around here. There's a girl your age staying with her grandpa on the farm next door. And another kid, Nick McKay is his name, may come, too. His parents work at the same hospital I do. His dad is with me in administration and his mom, Dr. Li, is a surgeon."

"Cool." Rebecca perked up. Kids her age sounded good.

"Jon?" Aunt Sylvie called from their bedroom. "Would you please get the laundry out of the dryer?"

"Sure." Uncle Jon rose to his feet. "Well, I'll leave you to check out the comics. Call me if you need anything."

Rebecca nodded. "Good night."

He left the room, closing the door behind him. Rebecca collapsed into her pillows. She shoved away the icky fact that Mom had discussed her secrets with Uncle Jon. This new information about Dad overshadowed everything else.

Usually she tried not to think about the fact that he was gone. She couldn't change it, and she and Mom were managing on their own, anyway. Sometimes, though, when Jenna's dad called Jenna "Precious Girl" or gently fixed one of her braids, a tiny hollow would open in Rebecca's heart. She'd remember the last time Dad took her trick-or-treating, and they'd laughed so hard about the funny face carved into the pumpkin across the street. Or she'd wish he was around to pitch to her, to help her practice her batting before a big softball game. She'd probably be a way better player if he was around to coach her. He'd been more of an athlete than Mom.

Rebecca always shut down these thoughts pretty fast. She hated getting sad.

But now she knew she and Dad had more in common than their appearance. They shared the same fascination with ghosts. Maybe he'd even passed it along to her. This was major. Lying there, Rebecca could almost feel a new thread of connection forming between her and Dad.

He was more than pictures and memories. She'd never really thought about it before, but Dad had once been twelve years old, just like her.

———

Thunder crashed. Rebecca shot upright out of a dead sleep.

She'd been dreaming about rain, about searching for something, but the images were already fading. It was dark, really dark around her. Where was the door, she couldn't find a door, there must be a door. She clutched the sheet, looking around wildly.

Shapes gradually came into focus. The rocking chair

in the corner, she'd seen that before. And the book lying on the floor, blood splatters shimmering faintly on its cover . . .

Rebecca flopped onto her back. That's right. She was in Iowa. She pressed her hand to her chest to calm herself. Everything was fine. Mom was here with her, they were visiting the Graffs and—

Her last conversation with Uncle Jon popped into her head.

Dad had stayed in this same room. Dad had believed in ghosts, too. She lifted her head from the pillow and peered past the nightstand. Sure enough, Dad's cardboard box was on the floor where she'd left it.

A burst of lightning lit the room, followed by the loudest boom of thunder Rebecca had ever heard. She braced herself for Justin's cries, but none came. A puff of wind brushed her face. Through a slight gap between the curtains, she noticed that the side window was open a crack. Weird. She remembered closing it before she went to sleep because Mom had said it was going to rain. Groaning, she rolled out of bed.

As she swept apart the curtains, Rebecca spied a small glowing circle far beyond the black expanse of cornfield. It was a security light shining over the neighbor's barn. But something else flickered beyond the silo, a tiny pinprick of light bobbing in the darkness. She squinted, trying to figure out what it could be.

Suddenly the wind rose and a blast of raindrops splattered against the pane, blotting out her view. A faint noise from outside reached her ears, a screech, maybe from an owl. She tilted her head, listening. Or was someone screaming?

Thunder rolled menacingly. When it was over, the screech was gone. Rebecca slammed the window shut, drew the curtains together, and scurried back to bed. Diving under the covers, she tried to shake off the disturbing suspicion that someone or something was out there sneaking around in the night.

FOUR

The next day, a Sunday, was spent getting ready for the barbecue. Rebecca played with Justin, grocery shopped with Uncle Jon, and baked cookies with Aunt Sylvie. When Mom asked about the box of Dad's things, Rebecca didn't tell her that he'd been into ghosts. For some reason, she wanted that to stay between her, Dad, and Uncle Jon for now, like a secret they shared. Happily, Uncle Jon didn't bring it up, either.

The humidity eased off and it ended up a perfect evening for a party, all warm breeze and washed-out blue sky. Uncle Jon arranged the two picnic tables in the middle of the backyard and set up lawn chairs in a semicircle. While everyone else was in the house changing clothes, Rebecca picked wildflowers for centerpieces and brainstormed things for her and the girl next door to do. They could play Frisbee, for sure. As she slid the flowers into a mason jar, the screen door squeaked open behind her.

"Co-Cap?" Mom called. "Is that what you're wearing?"

"Um, yeah." Rebecca had on her usual jean shorts and T-shirt. Mom, on the other hand, was dressed like she was going to a dance. She wore a new red checked sundress and her hair, usually in a ponytail, streamed down past her shoulders. Rebecca hastily tucked in her shirt. "This is just a barbecue, right?"

"Oh, it is, it is." Mom fiddled with the strap of her dress.

Aunt Sylvie, in yet another billowy maternity outfit, joined Mom on the porch. "Christine, you look fantastic," she trilled.

Rebecca slipped the final sprig of Queen Anne's lace into the jar and frowned. What did it matter what anyone looked like tonight?

"Divorced . . ." Aunt Sylvie lowered her voice. ". . . temporarily with his father . . ."

Rebecca's head snapped up, but before she could gather more intel, tires crunched on the gravel driveway. A rusted silver pickup drove into view and parked near the barn.

Aunt Sylvie clapped her hands together. "Our first

guests," she said. She grabbed Mom's elbow and pulled her to the driveway.

Two figures sat in the truck. The driver's-side door swung open, and a friendly-faced man with funky black-rimmed glasses climbed out. He carried a paper bag.

"Dad couldn't make it," he said, crossing to Aunt Sylvie, "but he sent some of his homegrown tomatoes."

"Wasn't that thoughtful." Aunt Sylvie took the bag in one hand and touched Mom's shoulder with the other. "Christine, this is Mark Schmidt. He grew up on the farm next door and is staying there with his dad this summer." Her gaze ping-ponged between them, a silly grin on her face.

Rebecca rolled her eyes as she walked to the driveway. Obviously this was the divorced guy, and her aunt was playing matchmaker. Mom never dated, though. She said she didn't have time for men, and no one could measure up to Dad, anyway. Mark, with his retro rock-band T-shirt and overpowering cologne, was trying too hard to be cool. Mom would see right through that. Poor guy.

But Mom tilted her head to one side, gold hoop earrings swinging. "Nice to meet you," she said to Mark, her voice breathy.

Rebecca almost gagged. Was her mother *flirting?*

"You two get acquainted, I'm going to go slice these tomatoes," Aunt Sylvie said, hustling to the house.

A tall girl about Rebecca's age stepped out of the pickup. She wore track shorts, a sparkly I LOVE LA shirt, and a major pout. Her stick-straight blond hair was pulled back so tightly in a barrette, Rebecca's scalp hurt just looking at it.

"About time you joined the party, Kelsie," Mark said. He nodded at Rebecca as she got to Mom's side. "Hi, there. Rebecca, right? My daughter is twelve, too."

"Great." Rebecca crossed her fingers behind her back. *Please be nice, please be fun.*

Kelsie took her time getting to the group. "Dad, I'm hungry." Her voice was high and whiny.

"I'm sure we'll eat soon," Mark said, draping an arm around her shoulder.

"Hi, Kelsie," Mom said brightly.

"Hello," Kelsie said sullenly. She scratched at a rash on her wrist. Dirt was caked under her fingernails.

Mom nodded at Mark's T-shirt. "I saw the White Stripes play in Chicago twenty years ago. Great concert."

"Really? I did, too." Mark beamed. "Maybe we were at the same show."

Rebecca tuned them out. "Wanna play Frisbee?" she asked Kelsie.

"Not really. It's too hot." Kelsie fanned herself with her hand.

"Oh. Okay, well how about croquet? Don't have to move much for that." Rebecca gave a little laugh.

"That's for old people," Kelsie said. "You guys have anything to drink or what?"

Rebecca's heart plummeted. "Sure, my aunt made lemonade. I'll bring it out."

As she retreated to the kitchen, she once again pictured Jenna, this time sitting around a campfire and eating s'mores with a ton of friendly girls their age.

The other kid that Uncle Jon mentioned, Nick, never showed up. Halfway through her burger at the kids' table, Rebecca gave up trying to talk to Kelsie. All she got were one-word answers. The little ones were much more entertaining, so Rebecca focused on them. It was fun to make them giggle. Kelsie ate silently, staring at her plate. Every once in a while she yawned.

After dinner, Rebecca organized a game of hide-and-seek for the little kids. Kelsie had no interest in playing along. Instead she wandered the backyard, digging at the ground with a stick. The adults hung out at one picnic table, Mom next to Mark, chatting away. The two of them were smiling a ton, which annoyed Rebecca. What could Mom find so interesting about him?

When the little kids started playing tag, Rebecca retreated to the swing with *Heart-Stopping Heartland Hauntings*. No one paid any attention to her. At one point, Kelsie sauntered past without saying a word and barged into the house, probably to use the bathroom. Rebecca's shoulders sagged with relief. She hadn't realized how tense Kelsie made her feel.

A blue SUV drove up the driveway. Rebecca peeked over the top of her book and watched Aunt Sylvie go meet the new arrivals. A petite Asian woman with glossy black hair and a preppy white man wearing khaki pants popped out of the car.

Rebecca went back to her book. She was starting a story entitled "The Violent Poltergeist of Valparaiso." The first line read:

Ghosts have emotions, exactly like people do. Some are sad. Some are angry.

Rebecca chewed on her thumbnail. A sad ghost she could probably handle. An angry one? That would be another story, especially if they could move things like a poltergeist. Those could get violent.

"My niece here plays softball!"

Rebecca looked up. Aunt Sylvie was steering a lanky boy in baggy basketball shorts and a baseball cap toward the swing.

"Becks, this is Nick McKay," Aunt Sylvie called. "He and his parents just came from his baseball game." She pointed toward the SUV Nick's parents had just left, then changed course and headed to the picnic table, leaving the boy slightly off-balance in front of the swing.

Rebecca cringed. Her aunt had shifted back into matchmaker mode. She closed her book, leaving a finger inside to mark the page. "Um. Hi."

"Hi." Nick's voice was unexpectedly raspy. Dark hair curled out from under his cap. He eyed his sneakers.

Rebecca's brain went blank. Nick said nothing. The silence between them stretched. Over by the barn, the little kids cracked up, almost like they could sense the awkwardness.

Rebecca's attention latched on to Nick's Los Angeles Dodgers shirt. "I'm a Cubs fan," she blurted.

"Why?" Nick raised an eyebrow. "They've had one good season in a hundred years."

"They've had more than that." Rebecca bristled. "Plus I live, like, twenty minutes north of Wrigley Field. The best park in baseball. I've been going to Cubs games my whole life." Nick didn't answer. She clicked her tongue.

"Why would you like the Dodgers? Have you ever lived in California?"

"No." Nick shrugged. "So?"

Laughter erupted from the picnic table. Uncle Jon was doing some sort of wacky impression.

"Oh-*kay*." Strike two. Between rude Nick and bratty Kelsie, Rebecca was done trying to make friends for the day. "I'm sure we'll have dessert soon. You don't have to hang here, feel free to go sit with your parents."

She buried her nose in *Heart-Stopping Heartland Hauntings*, scanning the same page over and over without making any sense of it. To her surprise, Nick didn't leave. He leaned against the tree trunk instead. Rebecca kept her feet on the ground and pushed back and forth in the swing. The ropes creaked against the branch above.

After a minute Nick spoke. "What are you reading?"

Rebecca kept her eyes on her book. "Ghost stories."

"Cool." He paused. "Are they scary?"

"Kind of."

"I'm more into comics."

"Really." Rebecca turned a page.

For a moment neither of them said anything. In the maple tree above, two squirrels noisily chased each other through the branches.

Finally, Nick cleared his throat. "You want some gum?"

Rebecca peered up at him. Between the growing twilight and the brim of his hat shielding his eyes, she couldn't read his expression. The gum could be a peace offering, though.

"Sure," she said.

Nick reached into his shorts pocket, withdrew a silver-wrapped rectangle, and offered it to her. The paper crackled as she peeled it away. She popped the gum into her mouth. Spearmint tingled her tongue.

"Thanks," she said.

"My brother thought he saw a ghost once," Nick said.

"Really?" Rebecca stopped swinging.

"Turns out it was only some fog in the yard." He gave her a half smile. Under the shadow of his hat, a dimple appeared in his cheek, completely throwing her off. It was adorable.

Rebecca tried not to gawk at it. "How old is your brother?"

"I've got two, actually. They're both nineteen. Twins."

"Huh. Cool." Rebecca wasn't quite ready to let him off the hook for dissing her, no matter how cute his dimple was. "Why didn't your parents force them to come here tonight, too?"

"Oh, they didn't force . . ." Nick took off his ball cap

and scratched his head, his dark hair going every which way. "Well, my brothers aren't around. They're both doing a summer semester at college. Yeah, uh, sorry I was kinda jerky before. Nothing against you."

"Okay." She waited.

"I'm in kind of a bad mood. My parents are being a pain."

Rebecca considered this. So she wasn't the only one having a tough night. She decided to accept his apology. "It's all right. I totally get it."

The screen door banged shut, and Kelsie slouched onto the back deck. When she spotted Nick, her posture changed, her chin going up and her shoulders pushing back. She straightened her barrette and clomped quickly down the stairs, coming right at the swing.

Rebecca closed her book. "What position do you play?" she asked Nick before Kelsie could kill the conversation.

"Shortstop," he said.

"No way. Me too . . . I mean, that's my favorite." She didn't have to mention how terrible she was at actually playing baseball. She grinned at him, and he grinned back. There was that dimple again.

Kelsie arrived and crossed her arms. "About time you showed up, Nick."

"Hi, Kelsie," Nick said.

"You two know each other?" Rebecca asked. She didn't like that idea at all.

"Yeah, from the pool," Kelsie said, keeping her focus on Nick. "Hey, if you're into the Dodgers, my mom is friends with one of the trainers. If you ever get out to L.A., she could totally get you tickets."

"Really?" Nick's eyes widened. "Awesome."

"No prob." Kelsie smiled coyly.

Heart-Stopping Heartland Hauntings slipped from Rebecca's lap and tumbled to the ground. Kelsie immediately bent and read the title.

"Wow." She sniffed. "You believe in that stuff?"

"Why not?" Rebecca said, swooping the book from the grass.

Kelsie rolled her eyes. "How about you, Nick?" Her fingers went to a gold necklace that peeked above her collar before disappearing under her T-shirt.

"I've never seen a ghost," he said.

"Of course you haven't." Kelsie snorted. "They aren't real."

Rebecca tightened her grip on the book. In the branches above, a mourning dove sang its sad song, the eerie notes soaring off into the corn.

"The stories can be cool, though," Nick said.

"Right?" Rebecca agreed. "I like learning the history behind them—"

"Who cares about history?" said Kelsie. "Bo-ring."

"Becks!" called Uncle Jon. "Would you mind getting the Popsicles for the little kids?"

"Sure." Rebecca stood and tucked the book safely under her arm. "Wanna help?" she asked Nick, purposefully not looking at Kelsie. She felt a little guilty about not including her, but, then again, why should she keep trying to be nice? Kelsie had made it clear she didn't want to be friends.

"Okay," said Nick.

"Not really," Kelsie said.

But as Rebecca and Nick went toward the house, she tagged along anyway. A sickly-sweet scent drifted around Kelsie—like her dad, she'd put on some kind of cologne or perfume. Rebecca snuffled a sneeze. She herself reeked of eau de bug spray. She noticed with satisfaction that Nick did, too.

As Rebecca opened the back door, Jade shot across the deck and dove into a bush under the kitchen window. Kelsie yelped.

"Whoa!" Nick said, admiration in his voice. "That's one fast cat."

"Right?" said Rebecca. "And she's missing an eye."

"Really?" Nick said. "Wild."

"That's disgusting," Kelsie said. All the color had drained from her cheeks. "I hate cats." She whirled around and stalked in the other direction, toward the picnic table.

"I like cats," Nick said.

Rebecca gave him a smile and ushered him into the kitchen. Since the evening air had cooled, the air-conditioning wasn't blasting and the windows were open. Party laughter floated inside. She flipped the light switch. The bulb overhead flashed and went out with a sharp crack, a tiny shower of sparks cascading over them. Rebecca jumped back, crunching Nick's foot. He sucked in a breath.

"Oh, sorry!" Rebecca said, mortified. "You okay?"

"Yeah, no biggie." Nick winced.

"Guess we need a new bulb." Rebecca bolted to the refrigerator; the imprint of the exploding light seared across her eyeballs. The glow from the open freezer barely penetrated the darkness in the kitchen. She grabbed two Popsicle boxes and held one out to Nick.

"Hope you like strawberry," she said.

Nick took a box. "Sure."

She closed the freezer door, and for a moment the kitchen went pitch-black. Before her eyes could adjust, the party talk outside faded away. A cold stillness dropped over her, reminding her of plunging deep underwater. A low buzz of energy fizzed in the air, invisible but unmistakably there. Uneasiness spread through her veins.

"Let's . . . go." Rebecca's mouth didn't seem to work right. It was a struggle to form words.

"Okay." Nick's voice sounded far-off.

Rebecca tried to move quickly, but crossing the kitchen took way too long, like she was stuck in slow motion. Panic rose in her chest. When her fingers finally touched the back door, a sight through the screen stopped her cold. In the gathering shadows under the maple tree, the wooden swing rocked back and forth. No one was anywhere near it. No breeze ruffled the air. Yet the swing swayed faster and faster, its ropes creaking ominously. Jade crouched nearby in the grass, watching it, ready to pounce.

"Nick, do you . . ." It was still hard for Rebecca to talk. "Do you see the swing?"

The moment the words were out of her mouth, the swing jerked to a stop. In a rush, the warm summer air and babble of party talk came back. The heaviness in the kitchen vanished.

Rebecca clutched Nick's arm. "You saw that, right?"

"Saw what?" Nick said. His voice wavered.

"The swing moving. By itself! And the air got all . . ." Rebecca couldn't quite describe it. "Weird?"

"I . . ." Nick trailed off. Then he shook his head. "I don't know what you're talking about."

"Hey, Becks!" Uncle Jon called. "You find the Popsicles?"

Nick squirmed out of Rebecca's grasp and pushed open the screen door. "Got 'em right here." He took off for the picnic tables.

Rebecca followed, her eyes on the now-motionless swing. As soon as Nick reached the others, the swing lurched back into action. Mom, Mark, and Kelsie, who had wedged herself between them at the table, were all facing the tree, but none of them reacted. Rebecca wanted to yell at them. Could no one else see what was happening?

"Dessert, kiddos!" Uncle Jon announced. The rocking swing was in his line of sight, too, but he didn't seem fazed at all.

Rebecca's gaze flew up the ropes that held the swing to the tree. Maybe a squirrel was up in the branches, biting at the knots. But there was nothing.

With a sudden, piercing yowl, Jade leapt at the swing and landed on the seat, making it rock violently. Then she sprang off and hurtled toward the back corner of the yard where the two cornfields met. Right before she got there, the cornstalks shook and parted, as if something invisible was trying to make room. Jade dove in after whatever it was. The corn swallowed her and snapped back into place.

Rebecca stood frozen in disbelief. What was going on? The party continued like nothing odd had happened at all. She scanned the others' faces. For a split second, it seemed Nick was watching the cornfield, too. But in the blink of an eye, he'd turned and continued to hand out Popsicles to the little kids.

Was she imagining it all? Or could there actually be something haunting the old Graff farm?

FIVE

Over the next few days, the household settled into a routine. Uncle Jon went to work, Mom wrote, and Aunt Sylvie spent time either at her part-time accounting job or resting in her room. Rebecca played with Justin, mostly inside, since a rainy spell started the day after the barbecue. In the evenings, they'd all watch the Cubs game on TV. Uncle Jon filled her in on the time Dad caught a ball in the bleachers at Wrigley and gave it to him. New little details about Dad were fun to hear. It was awesome to get to know the kid he'd once been.

The idea that the house might be haunted, though, overshadowed everything else. Rebecca kept on the lookout for any more unexplained phenomena. Nothing major happened, but plenty of little things did. She often got the sense someone was hovering behind her, except when she whirled around, there was never anyone there. Mysterious shadows moved out of the corner of her eye, only to evaporate when she faced them head-on. Once she accidentally brushed the knob of the door to the attic, and it was so cold her skin burned like she'd touched dry ice. Yet thirty seconds later when she gingerly tapped it again, the knob felt normal.

Rebecca was a big ball of nerves. On one hand, it was disturbing to get hit with unexpected scares. On the other hand, she'd always wanted to meet a real ghost— she should be excited it might actually be happening!

Every time she got frightened, she had to remind herself of that fact.

No one else seemed to pick up on anything strange. She didn't dare ask Uncle Jon or Mom about any of it, because he'd probably laugh and she'd probably scoff. Aunt Sylvie was no help either—the only thing she noticed was how jumpy Rebecca acted. If only she could talk to Jenna! Rebecca wrote her a letter filling her in on everything— Dad's box, Mom flirting, Kelsie, Nick, the creepy happenings, the whole story. Jenna would flip out.

Rebecca clung to the fact that she wasn't completely alone. There had been at least one other witness to the spooky stuff the night of the barbecue—Jade. She found a chapter in *Heart-Stopping Heartland Hauntings* entitled

"The Hellcat of Hickory Hills." It described a family pet that attacked its owners every time they opened the basement door, trying to keep them from going down there. They later discovered three human skeletons in the crawl space.

The story began:

Animals can sense evil. They can also sense spirits that are not meant to walk this earth. If a dog barks at empty air or a cat flees a room for no apparent reason, it means an unnatural, ghostly presence is near.

Rebecca couldn't get this idea out of her mind. What if the ghost wasn't just a ghost but an evil spirit? She searched high and low for Jade, but the cat had dropped out of sight since the barbecue. Hopefully nothing bad had happened to her after she'd gone into the corn.

One morning before Uncle Jon left for work, Rebecca mentioned that Jade hadn't been around.

"Oh, that cat goes missing from time to time. She'll come back once she gets hungry enough." He set his coffee cup in the sink.

Which reminded Rebecca: "Hey, is there a white cat around here, too?"

Uncle Jon was adjusting his tie. "Not that I've ever seen. Why?"

"Oh, I thought I saw one in the barn once." Rebecca

gave a little laugh like what she was about to say was no big deal. "Do you ever see things out of the corner of your eye?"

Uncle Jon shrugged. "Doesn't everybody on occasion? I mean, tricks of light happen, or insects whizz by and you think they're something they're not. Also, dare I say, sometimes people imagine things?" His mouth curled into a smile.

"Ha-ha," Rebecca said flatly. He was making fun of her.

Uncle Jon patted her arm. "I'm only teasing, Becks. You know that, right?" Rebecca nodded slowly. "All right. Gotta run. Hope it stops raining so you and Justin can get outside today. See you at dinner!"

He grabbed his car keys from a row of hooks by the back door and left. Rebecca sighed. She should've known better than to try to talk about anything supernatural again with Uncle Jon.

Her dad would've listened to her. But he wasn't around.

———

One evening the rain lifted at sunset, and the whole Graff family ventured to town for ice cream. The Tastee Shack was a small concrete building jammed with people hoping a frozen dessert would cool them off. Rebecca, Aunt Sylvie, and Justin got their cones first and exited the Shack to claim the only available picnic table on the sidewalk. As Rebecca took her first lick of her pistachio ice cream, a noisy herd of boys in baseball uniforms glided around the corner and onto the street in front of them.

"Isn't that Nick McKay?" Aunt Sylvie, seated next to her with Justin on her lap, pointed to the end of the pack.

Sure enough, Nick straggled along behind his teammates. Rebecca's heart rate picked up. Mom squeezed onto the bench on her other side.

"Nick, wait," called a whiny voice. Kelsie pedaled around the corner after him.

"Oh, and Mark's daughter." Mom raised her arm. "Hi, guys—"

"No!" Rebecca grabbed her elbow and pulled it down. "Stop! Please." The last thing she wanted was to be seen having ice cream with the family.

"What?" Mom looked confused.

Too late. Both Nick and Kelsie had seen them. He lifted his fingers from his handlebars in a little wave toward the Graff family.

Kelsie lowered her head and zoomed in front of him.

"Race you to the park!" she yelled. Nick immediately picked up his pace, chasing after her.

"He's such a nice kid," Aunt Sylvie said. "Maybe you should go watch one of his games sometime."

"Maybe," Rebecca said. She wasn't going to go unless Nick asked her to. It would be way too awkward otherwise. She wondered whether he'd invited Kelsie or if she'd shown up uninvited.

Uncle Jon dropped a fistful of napkins on the plastic table. "Actually, Nick's mom, Dr. Li, tells me he's really into old comic books. He'd probably like to come over and check out your dad's collection, Becks."

"That's a great idea," Sylvie said. "She also told me his best friend moved away last month and Nick's taken it pretty hard. I'm sure he'd appreciate an invitation. Justin, watch out!"

She swooped in with a napkin to catch Justin's scoop of mint chocolate chip right as it teetered off the cone. Justin giggled.

Rebecca swiped a dab of ice cream from her chin. So, Nick had lost his best friend for the summer, too. Her gaze followed him until he was gone.

———

In bed later that night, Rebecca cracked open *Heart-Stopping Heartland Hauntings*. She flipped to a chapter called "Do Not Disturb the Dead." It began:

Often a ghost is a spirit whose resting place has been disrupted.

This one was about a Nebraska library haunted by dozens of angry ghosts because it had been built atop a forgotten Native American burial ground.

Rebecca dozed off wondering if an ancient grave lay under the maple tree, its ghost furious that a swing dangled above it.

The next thing she knew, she was spinning around in pelting rain, black shapes thrashing around her, her stomach sick with dread. A scream shattered her eardrums, and a huge shadow fell straight at her—

She awoke with a gasp, tangled in sweaty sheets. She opened her mouth to call Mom, then clamped it shut. She was too old for that. Instead, she stared at the ceiling, willing her heart to slow.

When she was little, Rebecca had had nightmares all the time. Bizarre, terrible ones about cackling green skeletons or spiders the size of a couch. She'd wake up crying. Sometimes Dad would come comfort her, but mostly it was Mom who would rush in and gather her into her arms. She'd make Rebecca describe the dream, then ask silly questions like "Now, was this skeleton pea green or Christmas-tree green?" or "When the spider tapped on the window, did all eight feet wear tap shoes?" Rebecca always ended up in a fit of giggles, her fear forgotten.

As she'd grown, she'd learned a cool trick. In the middle of a nightmare, she could make herself realize she was dreaming. A sense of calm would settle over her, and she could actually feel her mom's hand pressing gently on her shoulder, reassuring her that all was well. Then she could wake herself up. The nightmares stopped.

Rebecca rubbed her forehead. She hadn't realized she was stuck in a bad dream this time, which was unusual. So what had made her wake up? A sliver of moonlight showed between the curtains, which meant the sky was at least partially clear and no noisy storm had bothered her.

She needed water. As she reached for her glass on the nightstand, she froze, her arm hanging in midair. The rocking chair in the corner was facing the wall. She stared at it. Had she moved it earlier and forgotten? But why would she have done that? It looked unnatural, so ominous, so . . . wrong. As she watched, the chair seemed to twitch. What if it began to rock, pick up speed, scuttle right at her—

Rebecca squeezed her eyes shut tight and counted to ten. When she looked again, the chair was turned around, back in its usual spot. She blinked. How had that happened? Or had the chair never been out of place? Either way, she couldn't trust her own eyes.

Rebecca pulled the covers tight under her chin. Little creepy incidents kept occurring, but none of it added up. She hadn't actually SEEN a ghost. She had no proof one existed.

She was beginning to wonder if something was wrong with her.

That was almost scarier than the thought of a real ghost.

six

Rebecca woke up later than usual the next morning. The sun shone brightly through the lace curtains, its cheerful glow almost wiping away her dark memories of the night before. She threw on a pair of shorts and a Cubs T-shirt and padded downstairs, surprised Mom hadn't knocked on her door earlier. No one was around. On the kitchen table she found a note.

Let you sleep in—today, at least!! Jon's at work and Sylvie took Justin to a mommy-and-me class. When they get home, could you please watch Justin for a bit? Breakfast stuff on the counter. Come say hi—I'm in my glamorous office!! —Mom

Typical caffeinated Mom. Rebecca definitely hadn't inherited her morning-person gene. Groggily she took one of Justin's apple juice boxes from the refrigerator and grabbed a poppy seed muffin from a plate on the counter. She leaned over the sink to snarf her breakfast, letting the crumbs fall wherever they wanted to. It'd be awesome to have some time by herself, but she had to admit Justin was growing on her. He wiggled with joy whenever she walked into a room.

Outside the window puffy clouds glided lazily across the sky. Rebecca's attention wandered to the old maple tree.

Jade sat motionless on the swing, staring straight at her.

Goose bumps stung the back of Rebecca's neck. The cat hopped to the ground and slinked to the corner of the yard where the cornfields met, stopping at the exact spot where she'd disappeared the night of the barbecue. The exact spot where something else had gone into the corn.

Jade peered over her shoulder at the house, as if she was waiting for someone.

Waiting for her.

Rebecca's mind raced. Could Jade possibly know that she, too, had witnessed the swing rock by itself and the corn shake? It was like the cat was trying to communicate, asking Rebecca to follow her into the field. Rebecca crumpled the empty juice box in her hand and swallowed her fear. This was her chance. She needed to find out if she had an overactive imagination, like Mom said, or if there truly was a ghost.

She threw the juice box in the trash, jammed on her sneakers, and rushed out the back door. Jade yowled and vanished into the corn. When Rebecca reached the field, she spotted the cat far down the path and sped after her. The corn scratched Rebecca's bare legs and arms, and sweat trickled between her shoulder blades, but she didn't care. She pushed away her fear of getting lost in the field. She couldn't lose Jade.

The cat zigged and zagged in and out of the rows of corn, always reappearing right when Rebecca thought she was gone for good. Her heart pounded in her ears. She accidentally barreled through a cloud of gnats and a bunch invaded her mouth. Spitting and swiping at her face, she kept on until finally the path dead-ended at a waist-high wire fence. Jade slipped underneath, veered right, and scampered uphill through a stretch of weeds to a line of trees. Rebecca parted the middle two wires, slid between them, and resumed the chase.

Water splashed ahead. On the other side of the trees the ground dipped to a small hollow where a creek flowed, its path a squiggle of curves. Jade had already crossed and trotted into some woods. Rebecca tried to clear the creek in one jump but landed in water up to her ankles, soaking her sneakers. The shock of cold water felt awesome, but she couldn't stick around to enjoy it. She kept after Jade.

In the woods the air was hushed, the ground choked by underbrush and decaying leaves. Rebecca couldn't find a trail but caught sight of Jade's black tail sliding around a tree trunk ahead. She scrambled forward over thick roots and fallen branches, the ground angling uphill, until she emerged from the woods and landed in someone's backyard. She stopped dead in her tracks.

At least, it used to be someone's yard. Now it was a mass of tangled weeds and rusted farm equipment. Under a clump of enormous trees sat a ruined building. Faded gray exterior, boarded-up windows, a sagging roofline— an old, abandoned farmhouse.

Rebecca's senses tingled. This was cool. But creepy. A crumbling barn squatted to her right, blue sky showing through yawning holes in the roof. She picked her way through the weeds and came across two overgrown tire tracks that must've once been a driveway. They led between the house and the barn, then took a curve and disappeared.

She continued toward the house. Chips of white paint clung to the siding, vines curled up the window frames, loose boards dangled. She circled around to the front. The whole building drooped to one side under the point of a steep roof. Parts of the porch railing had rotted, leaving jagged chunks of wood hanging like teeth. A splintered crack cut across the top of the front door.

The place must have been empty for years. Not only was it falling apart, but there were no toys or lawn chairs in the yard, no cars parked in the driveway, not a single NO TRESPASSING sign. In fact, there was no sign of life at all. Even the birds had quit singing. Rebecca felt utterly alone.

She hastily backtracked to the rear of the house where a tiny one-story addition had been tacked on, a dilapidated afterthought. One of its walls had caved in, and a scraggly dead bush poked up through the debris. Something glinted near its roots. Her heart surged with fear. It was an eyeball.

Meow.

Rebecca clamped a palm to her chest. The eye belonged to Jade, watching her. The cat backed away, then edged past a door hanging by one hinge and snaked into the house.

Rebecca hesitated. Who knew what she'd find inside this ruined place? But she'd come too far to turn back. She climbed over the fallen siding, through the doorway, and into a kitchen. Cracked pipes stuck out from one wall, the sink they'd been attached to long gone. Dark water spots marred the ceiling. Decades of scratches etched the stained linoleum floor, and the air reeked of mildew. Jade was nowhere to be seen.

Holding her nose, Rebecca went deeper inside the house, her wet sneakers squeaking in the quiet. The next room seemed older, with high ceilings and a hardwood floor. There was no furniture. Boards covered the windows, letting little light in. A clot of cobwebs jiggled in one corner. Shuffling closer, she spied a fat black spider inching sluggishly toward a quivering white bundle. She shuddered and passed into the front room.

To her right gaped a blackened fireplace, only half its wooden mantel still intact over the hearth. Ahead was the front door. To her left a staircase rose to the second floor.

An empty loneliness washed over Rebecca. Who had lived here? Why had they left? The house was so bleak and alone, it was like a whole other world. Beyond one empty window frame, prairie grasses and wildflowers trembled outside in the breeze. But the wind didn't reach inside. Instead, the air hung motionless around her.

A thump and a meow came from overhead. Jade.

The stairs creaked when Rebecca stepped on them,

but they were solid under her feet. As she climbed higher, the smell of wet, rotten wood grew. A row of muddy paw prints led her to an upstairs hallway with four open doorways and into a small front bedroom. Jade waited on a narrow seat built into an alcove under a window.

On one side of the room, the ceiling sloped almost to the floor, several strips of colorless wallpaper spiraling off the slanting surface. A doorless closet stood in one corner, empty except for dust and dirt. As Rebecca neared the window, Jade bounded off the seat and scuttled past her into the hall.

Rebecca knelt on the window seat and pressed her right palm against the wavy glass pane. In the middle of the front yard, a huge twisted oak stretched to the sky. Through its leaves and a screen of pines behind it she could make out yet another cornfield and a tiny patch of road. A red van silently cruised into view and was gone. The house must be almost completely hidden from whatever traffic drove by, a forgotten island in the ocean of corn.

And she was alone inside it. No one knew where she was. A chill crawled across her skin. If anything happened to her, no one was around to help. Her hand dropped from the window, leaving a print on the pane.

Suddenly the air grew thick and cold. Rebecca puffed

out a breath, and a wisp of fog twirled from between her lips. From behind her came a bloodcurdling hiss. She twisted around. Jade crouched in the hall staring past her, hackles bristling along her spine like a Mohawk. An icy breeze brushed Rebecca from behind. She slowly turned back to the window.

Her handprint was a smudge on the pane. Next to it another handprint was forming, identical in size.

Another *right* handprint.

Rebecca pushed off the window seat and staggered backward. Something invisible hovered in front of her, next to her, behind her—everywhere. Panic flooded her body.

There was a ghost. She was in a room with a ghost. She knew it 100 percent in her bones. And she was terrified.

Rebecca staggered through the dense air toward the door, finally breaking free in the hall. As she hit the stairs something rustled behind her, but she didn't stop to see what it was. She dashed down the steps and threw her body at the front door, smacking it wide open. She stumbled across the porch, hurtled to the ground, and ripped through the tall weeds to the driveway, away from whatever was behind her and toward safety. Following the tire tracks around the trees, she spotted the country road in the distance and doubled her speed. She'd almost reached it when her foot caught on a root and she fell hard. Her hands and knees smashed into the gravel, a spray of rocks flying up on either side of her.

"Whoa!" someone yelled. Bike brakes squealed. "What the—?"

Rebecca, numb with shock, raised her head. A few feet away from her in the middle of the road, Nick straddled a mountain bike.

"Are . . . are you okay?" he sputtered.

Rebecca gasped. "Yeah," she said, the word catching in her throat. Her hands stung, and her knees were streaked with blood. Tears pricked her eyes.

Nick dumped his bike by the side of the road. "Here, let me help you," he said, hurrying to her with his hand out.

Rebecca struggled to her feet before he reached her. He grabbed her elbow as she swayed.

"Geez, why are you so cold?" He glanced at her bleeding knees. "Oh, you're hurt."

"It's no big deal." She was panting.

Nick raised his eyebrows. "Are you sure?"

"I was just . . . I was back there in that house and I . . ." Rebecca's voice trailed off. She wasn't sure how to explain what had just happened.

Jade streaked past them, crossed the road, and plunged into a ditch. Nick dropped Rebecca's elbow. She immediately missed the warmth of his hand.

"It's that cat again," he said. "Jade, right? Don't tell me you were running away from her."

"No, I was chasing her. She led me right to that house. And I swear I felt . . . and then I saw . . ." Rebecca craned around, searching for the bedroom window. From where they stood only a bit of roof was visible behind the trees.

Nick's mouth twisted. "Are you sure that scary book you're reading isn't messing with your mind?"

"What?" Rebecca said. "No!"

"Have you ever heard of the power of suggestion?" His reasonable tone was maddening. "Like, when you start thinking about something and suddenly you see it everywhere, whether it is there or not?"

"That is not what this is," Rebecca snapped. "What are you doing here, anyway?"

Nick held up his hands innocently. "Hey, I was biking by, minding my own business, and you wiped out right in front of me."

Rebecca's cheeks burned. If only she could run away and disappear like Jade. She bent over and brushed off bits of gravel stuck to her knees. "What's the deal with this place?"

"No clue," Nick said. "It's been empty as long as I can remember. It's . . ." He stopped.

Rebecca straightened, searching his face. "It's creepy, isn't it?"

His eyes flickered with uneasiness. "I guess."

Now that he'd admitted that, she sensed an opening. "Hey, you remember when we were getting Popsicles in my uncle's kitchen the other night?"

"Yeah." Nick gave her a wary look.

"Did you feel the air get all weird? Like heavy? And cold?"

"Um . . ." Nick shuffled his feet. "Well, my dad says sometimes you can feel the barometric pressure drop before it rains."

Rebecca crossed her arms. "Really. I've never felt anything that intense before. Plus, it didn't rain that night." Nick's gaze shifted to the ground. She pressed on. "Did you see the swing moving by itself? And then Jade attacked it?"

"I don't know. I mean, I saw the cat jump on the swing." He wouldn't meet her eyes. He was definitely hiding something.

"And then she ran off into the field and the cornstalks, like, moved to make way for her!"

"I . . . Nope. I don't know what you're talking about." Nick backed away from her toward the road. "Look, I gotta go."

"Wait—" Rebecca's phone beeped. "Seriously? This thing works here but barely at my uncle's house?" She fished it from her back pocket.

Nick picked up his bike. "Cell service around here is messed up."

Rebecca read the text. It was from Mom. *Where r u? S & J r home.* Shoot. Aunt Sylvie and Justin were home and it was time to babysit. She thrust the phone into her pocket. Nick was already astride his bike.

"Where are you going?" she asked.

"I'm late. I've gotta mow the McGintys' yard. You seem fine now." He pushed up on the seat and began to pedal away.

"But—"

Nick half swiveled. "I think you should stay away from meadow winds."

"What's that supposed to mean?" Rebecca called.

Nick pointed over his shoulder. "Read the sign."

Rebecca turned. Running parallel to the property along the edge of the road was a low, battered fence. A bright orange STAY OUT sign hung from one post. Underneath it was a small, weathered plaque. Its words, in faded red paint, were barely legible.

MEADOW WINDS FARM.

SEVEN

Playing trucks with Justin in the backyard that afternoon, Rebecca couldn't get Meadow Winds Farm out of
her mind. It was possible she'd been in the same room
with an actual ghost . . . and she'd blown it. She'd freaked
out and run away.

She'd never forgive herself.

When she and Jenna thought there was a ghost in
the Alvarados' house the summer before, she hadn't been
scared. She'd been thrilled. She'd marched right up to the
window in the dark, practically daring a ghost to appear.
She'd gone after it like a boss.

Of course, it ended up there hadn't really been a
ghost. Maybe she'd suspected that all along, and that was
why she had been so calm. This was different. Something
was definitely there. That handprint had convinced her it

wasn't all in her mind. There was no way she had imagined that.

But facing a real ghost was way scarier than she'd ever dreamed.

As she pushed the plastic bulldozer through the grass after Justin's fire truck, Rebecca made a promise to herself. The next time anything ghostly happened, no way would she be a scaredy-cat.

If there was a next time.

Uncle Jon got home from work around five thirty, and Justin happily accompanied him into the house. Alone in the backyard, Rebecca found herself drawn to the swing. Locusts buzzed their deafening song from the branches above, the sound reminding her of the sizzle of raw bacon hitting a hot pan over and over. The swing didn't move. She wrapped her fingers around one of its ropes.

Somewhere beyond the cornfield ahead lurked the mysterious abandoned farmhouse. Jade had led her there. The handprint had appeared there. But why? Rebecca closed her eyes, hoping for the heavy underwater feeling to rush her, for time to slow, for a ghost to materialize next to her . . .

"Hey, Co-Cap!"

Rebecca startled and her hand scudded down the rough rope, hurting her scraped palm.

Mom was crossing the yard from the barn. "What have you been doing all day?"

Rebecca opened her mouth. She wanted to spill everything—the shaking corn, the mysterious house, the strange handprint—but Mom wouldn't want to hear it. Dad probably would've. A thought crossed her mind. Maybe Mom had no clue Dad had been obsessed with ghosts when he was young. Maybe if she did know, she'd be more understanding of Rebecca now. Then she might listen and help her figure out what was going on.

"Not much." Rebecca gave her a sidelong glance. "Hey. Did you know Dad was into ghosts when he was a kid, just like me?"

Mom blinked rapidly. "Oh. Who told you that?"

"Uncle Jon. He said Dad even wrote away to a paranormal society once." Rebecca watched her mom's face closely.

Mom pursed her lips. "Huh. Well, it's common for kids to be interested in that stuff. Anyway, on another topic." She paused and smoothed her hair. "I have a question for you."

Rebecca winced. Once again, Mom was shutting her down. She shouldn't have expected anything different. "Okay," she said dully.

Mom beamed. "What do you think of Mark?"

Rebecca scrambled to switch gears. "Huh?"

"Come on." Mom playfully nudged Rebecca with her elbow. "Mark Schmidt from the farm next door. You met him at the barbecue?"

"Oh. Yeah." Rebecca leaned down to pluck a clover from the grass, trying to ignore the sparkle in Mom's eyes. They'd just been talking about Dad; how could Mom be so excited about Mark? "He's fine."

"I know you and Kelsie didn't really hit it off, but try to give her a break. Mark says the divorce has been really hard on her."

"Okay." Rebecca studied the clover, twirling it between her thumb and forefinger.

Mom sighed. "There aren't many girls your age around here. We think you two should go to a movie sometime."

Rebecca scrunched up her face. *We?* Either Mom and Mark had discussed this at the barbecue or they'd talked since. Either way, the thought made her squirm. "Um, Kelsie was not interested in being my friend. Believe me."

"Maybe she's shy," Mom said. "She's lonely, I'm sure. Put yourself in her shoes. Her mom's living in LA, her dad's temporarily unemployed—"

"You're right," Rebecca agreed, so they could stop talking about Kelsie. "So what's for dinner?"

"Don't know. But the reason I bring up the Schmidts

is because Mark called to ask a favor. He and his father have a meeting tonight, so he wondered if Kelsie could eat with us. She'll be here soon. Come on, let's go help Jon." Mom linked arms with Rebecca and pulled her along toward the house.

Rebecca's mood dropped like a sinker ball.

———

Within an hour, everyone had gathered around the kitchen table. Kelsie had arrived with a sullen expression and dark circles under her eyes. As late-day sunlight streamed through the window and Justin rolled peas around his red plastic plate, Mom asked Kelsie all sorts of questions. She was obviously trying to draw her out of her shell.

It worked. Turned out, Kelsie liked to show off. She rambled on and on about her soccer medals and her amazing grades. All the adults oohed and ahhed. And she kept shooting glances at Rebecca to make sure she'd heard all the achievements and praise. It was beyond annoying. Rebecca tuned out. She was dying to bring up Meadow Winds and see what Uncle Jon knew about it. But she couldn't get a word in. Instead, she picked at her food and beat herself up about how she'd messed up earlier, not only fleeing from the ghost but falling on her face in front of Nick. Two epic fails.

"Becca, smile," Justin demanded, breaking into her thoughts. He blew her a kiss across the table. Her heart warmed. She blew one back.

"My mom has a cool new condo in L.A.," Kelsie was saying. "It's in a high-rise and all modern."

"That sounds neat," Mom said.

"Yeah, I can't wait to visit." Kelsie pouted. "I hate these old houses."

Rebecca's eyes darted to Aunt Sylvie and Uncle Jon. Kelsie had basically insulted her hosts. But Aunt Sylvie only sipped her milk, and Uncle Jon tilted his head thoughtfully.

"Oh, I don't know," he said, wiping his mouth with a napkin. "These older homes are a lot of work, but they have great character. I think William Foxx did a pretty good job on this one."

"Who?" Mom asked, emptying the pitcher of water into her glass. "I thought a Graff built this house."

"We did, too, until we saw the original paperwork," said Aunt Sylvie.

Rebecca perked up. History was tons more entertaining than Kelsie's bragging.

"Apparently, William Foxx was my great-something-grandfather." Uncle Jon pushed his chair away from the table. "His only child—Caroline, I think?—married a German immigrant named Thomas Graff. That's where the Graff name came from. Then Caroline and Thomas inherited this house when William died." He rose with the empty pitcher.

Rebecca straightened in her chair. There was so much she didn't know about her dad's side of the family.

"Caroline's a pretty name," Aunt Sylvie said, rubbing her belly. "I have a feeling this one could be a girl."

"That'd be so exciting, Sylvie," Mom said.

"Don't count on it," Uncle Jon said, filling the pitcher at the sink. "We Graffs tend to have boys. In fact, Rebecca, you're the first girl born into the family in four generations."

Kelsie yawned, clearly bored, and shoved a forkful of pasta into her mouth. Rebecca seized her chance.

"Speaking of old houses," she said, waving her hand in the direction she'd traveled with Jade. "What's with that wrecked house on the other side of the fields?"

Kelsie froze mid-chew, her eyes wide.

"You mean Meadow Winds Farm?" Uncle Jon asked.

"Uh, yeah," Rebecca said. "Looks like no one has lived there in a long time."

"What's this? An empty house?" Mom frowned.

"Go outside?" Justin asked.

"When we're all done, honey," Aunt Sylvie said, gently wiping off his milk mustache.

"When I was little, an older couple lived there." Uncle Jon carried the pitcher to the table and took his place in his chair.

"Who were they? Was the house run-down back then, too? Have you ever been inside?" Rebecca couldn't stop her questions from gushing out.

"No, no, not at all." Uncle Jon laughed. "The Turners were mean. Ben and I got in big trouble for even fishing on their side of the creek." He poured Mom more water.

Kelsie flipped her ponytail. "Actually, Meadow Winds belongs to my family." All eyes focused on her. She smiled smugly, obviously glad to be the center of attention again.

"Wait." Rebecca went still. "What?"

"Is that right?" Uncle Jon said.

"Yes. And my grandpa used to rent the house out a long time ago. So whoever those Turner people were, they didn't own it." Kelsie tossed her napkin on her plate.

"But it's empty now?" Mom asked.

"Yeah, I guess he and his cousin have been fighting over the land for, like, ever. It's worth a ton of money." Kelsie rubbed part of the gold chain visible around her neck, the rest of it tucked once again under her shirt. "Once my grandpa owns it himself, he'll sell it and we'll be rich." She smirked.

What a bragger. Rebecca stabbed her last piece of rotini with her fork.

"Rebecca, you didn't go inside that house, did you?" Mom asked, narrowing her eyes.

"Uh . . ." Rebecca stuffed the pasta into her mouth, trying to buy time.

Bang! Bang! Bang! Justin pounded his spoon on the table.

"Please stop that, sweetie," said Aunt Sylvie.

"I know you might be tempted to explore, Rebecca," Mom continued. "But if the house hasn't been occupied in years, it could be dangerous."

Bang! Bang! Bang!

"No, Justin." Uncle Jon took away the spoon. Rebecca kept her eyes on her plate. Maybe Justin had derailed the conversation.

"The floors might be rotted and you could fall through and get hurt." Mom would not let it go. "Or animals could be living in there."

"That's true," Kelsie said, bobbing her head up and down. "My dad almost got bit by a ginormous snake there once. You need to stay out of there, Rebecca."

Rebecca gritted her teeth. Kelsie couldn't tell her what to do.

"Outside!" Justin yelled. "Pitty pease!"

Uncle Jon pushed his chair back from the table. "I tell you what, if everyone is done, why don't we go sit on the front porch? We can watch this little fella run off some energy in the yard." He lifted Justin out of his booster seat.

"Yes, please," Aunt Sylvie said.

Everyone else got up, and Rebecca finally breathed easier. Justin for the save. She really didn't feel like hanging out with Kelsie, though. "I'll clear the table."

"That's sweet of you, thanks," Aunt Sylvie said.

"So, my dad should be picking me up soon, right?" Kelsie asked.

"Think so," Mom answered.

As everyone filed out of the kitchen, Rebecca began gathering the silverware and piling the empty plates on top of one another. The front door opened and closed, and then she was alone. Thank goodness. She didn't know how much more Kelsie she could stand.

There was a footstep in the hall. Rebecca looked up. Kelsie leaned in the doorway.

"You really shouldn't trespass on Schmidt property," she said. Her smile was sugary-sweet, but her eyes were cold. "If I ever catch you, I'll tell my grandpa. And he'll call the police." Before Rebecca could form an answer, Kelsie stalked into the hall and out the front door.

Rebecca snatched the dirty dishes from the table and stomped to the sink. Kelsie made her so mad. How could Nick be friends with someone like her? Through the kitchen window the leaves of the maple tree twitched and the swing swayed gently in a light breeze. Rain clouds gathered far off on the horizon.

All of a sudden, the temperature in the kitchen took a nosedive, and a low buzz filled her ears. A garbled whisper bounced around the walls and retreated. Shocked, Rebecca dropped the plates in the sink, but they barely made a clatter. The air pressed in on her from all sides, pinning her feet in place. She twisted around, searching for the source of the sounds, and saw nothing unusual. The whisper repeated, this time from the window only inches from her head. Mustering all her strength, Rebecca heaved herself away from the sink and a sight outside caught her eye.

Where the footpath went into the field, the cornstalks that moments ago had been upright and whole were now broken and trampled. As she stared in disbelief, an eerie scream replaced the whisper, seemingly coming from the depths of the corn. Another scream joined in, two discordant screeches rising higher and higher. Rebecca clapped her hands over her ears and screwed her eyes shut.

The front door opened with a muted bang. The screams died away. The air snapped back to normal. Rebecca gasped with relief and checked outside. The corn stalks stood straight and tall, no signs of destruction anywhere.

"Becks, do the dishes later," called Uncle Jon. "Come on out."

She couldn't leave the kitchen fast enough.

EiGHT

Rebecca slept with her door wide open that night. As much as she wanted to communicate with the ghost, she needed a clear escape route, just in case. Plus, it made her feel less cut off from the rest of the family. What had happened in the kitchen freaked her out. This ghost wasn't playing. Maybe it was mad she had run out of the house when she saw the second handprint. It seemed to want her to go back to Meadow Winds. But why? Trying to understand the motivations of a real ghost was way more complicated than reading about them in books.

To her surprise, she slept through the night. Both the whispers and the nightmares had stayed away. Rebecca didn't know whether to be relieved or bummed.

Unfortunately, the rain had returned. Rebecca and

Justin were stuck inside alone all morning playing with toys and watching cartoons. Aunt Sylvie came home for the afternoon. As she headed upstairs to put Justin to bed for his nap, she called over her shoulder to Rebecca.

"Becks, it looks like it's stopped raining for now. Would you please go get the mail?" Her mouth twitched, like she was trying not to smile. Which wasn't unusual. Rebecca was learning that Aunt Sylvie was one of those always-look-on-the-bright-side people, like Jenna.

"Sure." Rebecca slipped into her flip-flops. She should be more optimistic, too. It'd be good to get out of the house, even for a few minutes. Maybe today she'd finally get a letter from Jenna.

The mailbox was mounted to a wooden post next to the road. Gulping in the fresh air, Rebecca zigzagged along the driveway, dodging a million puddles. Sure enough, the mailbox was stuffed with catalogs and letters. She quickly sorted through the pile and found a small blue envelope with familiar handwriting. A letter from Jenna—yes! She hugged the rest of the mail to her chest and ripped open the envelope.

It was only one page, basically a list of all the awesome activities and fun people at Camp Birchdale. Rebecca couldn't believe it. Not only did Jenna seem totally fine without her but she didn't seem to know anything about the ghost. Their letters must've crossed in the mail.

There was a note at the bottom of the page.

P.S. There's a boy here named Max with the cutest smile.

An image of Nick popped into Rebecca's head. She doubted Max could be cuter.

Bike brakes squealed next to her.

"Hey," said Nick. "What's up?"

Rebecca crumpled Jenna's letter and shrank back against the mailbox. He couldn't read her mind, could he? "What? I got a letter from my friend."

"A letter, huh?" Nick raised an eyebrow. "That's kinda old-school."

"She's at sleepaway camp. No electronics," Rebecca said defensively.

Nick lifted his hands in surrender. "Okay, okay, I didn't mean anything."

"Oh." Of course. Rebecca stepped away from the mailbox and tried to act casual. "What are you doing here?"

"Looking for you, actually." He took off his helmet and swiped his hand across his forehead. His dark hair stuck up all over. Adorable.

Rebecca's mouth went dry. "Really?"

"Yeah, didn't your aunt tell you? She called my dad this morning and said I should come over and check out some old comics you have."

Oh. Rebecca deflated. Aunt Sylvie had set this up. It hadn't been his idea at all. "Right."

"Plus, it's really boring at home," Nick continued. "My parents are always at the hospital and my brothers are gone. And my friend Matt moved, so . . ."

"Got it." Geez, he'd made his point; he had nothing better to do. But then she remembered how bad it was to be without your best friend. Plus, since Jenna was like a sister to her, she understood the sibling thing. She gave him a pass. "Come on."

They rambled up the driveway, Nick pushing his bike along. Neither of them spoke for a minute. Rebecca thought about bringing up Meadow Winds, but that might remind him of her clumsy fall. She'd embarrassed herself enough already.

"So," Nick said, breaking the silence. "My dad says your mom is writing something?"

"Yeah." Rebecca relaxed. This topic was safe. "She's working on her dissertation for her PhD. She's an English teacher. At a high school."

"Cool." Nick kicked a piece of gravel. "My brother Tim wants to be a teacher. My parents want him to be a doctor, though."

"What about your other brother?"

"Trevor? He's not sure yet." A sad note crept into his voice.

"You miss them?" Rebecca asked.

"Heck yeah. They're the ones who usually come to my baseball games and cheer me on. My parents aren't that into sports."

The front door opened, and Aunt Sylvie stepped onto the porch. She held Dad's box in her arms. "Well, look who's here! So glad you could stop by, Nick."

A pitcher of lemonade and two glasses perched on a table between two wicker rocking chairs. Wow, Aunt Sylvie had really set the scene. Rebecca squirmed inwardly, hoping Nick didn't think this was all too nerdy. Also, Dad's comics could be totally lame for all she knew.

"Hi, Mrs. Graff," Nick said, leaning his bike against the house.

"Here are the comics." Aunt Sylvie set the box on the porch floor. "Thought you could look at them out here, so your voices don't wake Justin. Actually, I'm going to take a nap, too." She placed her hands on her back and stretched.

"Okay. Thanks," Rebecca said.

"Have fun, kids." Aunt Sylvie slipped into the house, but not before she winked over her shoulder at Rebecca. Rebecca shot a glance at Nick to see if he noticed. Luckily, he was busy pouring a glass of lemonade.

"So, what's the deal with your dad?" he asked.

"Oh." Rebecca tucked a curl behind her ear and took a deep breath. She should've expected this question. "He died when I was in kindergarten."

Nick's expression shifted from curiosity to shock. The "in kindergarten" part always got to people. "Sorry, I didn't know. I thought your parents were divorced or something."

"It's fine," Rebecca said, automatically giving the same answer she always did when anyone asked about Dad. People usually got sad for her, and then she felt like it was her job to comfort them. She hated that. "I mean, I'm not sad all the time or anything."

Nick clunked his glass on the table and awkwardly swiped his palms on his T-shirt. "Your mom seems cool, though."

"She's fine. Usually." Rebecca pointed at the box, more than ready to change the subject. "Go ahead."

Nick blew out a breath, obviously relieved. "Yeah, great. Okay." He opened the cardboard flaps and whistled. "Awesome—*The Amazing Spider-Man* number 229!"

Whew. Rebecca sank into the other rocking chair while he dug through the box. Her eyes drifted out to the road.

Visiting the farm and learning what Dad was like as a kid made her realize even more what she was missing. Not only did she not have a dad in general, but she also didn't have *him*. Her own dad. The guy who shared her love of the Cubs. The guy who knew that the scar on her left shin was from falling off her tricycle when she was three. The guy who loved pistachio ice cream, just like she did, even though nobody else in the world seemed to.

"Uh, Rebecca." Nick's voice cut into her thoughts.

"What?" It took her a second to come back to reality. Nick's eyes were wide.

He held out a creased envelope. "Is this yours?"

She took it. The envelope was addressed to her dad at the farm and postmarked years before. She quickly did the math. It must've been from the last summer he'd stayed in Iowa. The return address was a Chicago one she didn't recognize. She flipped over the envelope. Sloppy block letters—her dad's handwriting—scrawled across the back.

SIGNS OF THE GHOST

Rebecca gasped. Her eyes raced down the page.

1. The swing moves by itself
2. Air gets freezing cold, feels weird (static?)
3. Shadows move out of the corner of my eye
4. Corn shakes

All this happens at Grandpa Sam's house,
    usually when it rains.

And when I bike by Meadow Winds Farm, I get
    a bad feeling some THING is watching me.

GOAL: Be brave. Find out what it wants.

Rebecca gripped the arm of her chair, the wicker digging into her palm. "Where'd this come from?"

"In here." Nick passed her a *Batman* comic. "So it's not yours?"

"No! My dad must've written this when he was a kid. Look, it's the same!" Rebecca laid the envelope against the top of the box to show him her dad's handwriting samples side by side.

"Whoa," Nick said.

"I told you something spooky was going on!" Excitement bubbled inside of her. "This is proof!"

"I don't know about proof—"

"Yes, it is! And it's not only me who thinks so!" That reminded her, he'd totally been hiding something when she'd asked him about the ghost before. Rebecca narrowed her eyes. "*Now* will you admit you saw weird stuff the night of the barbecue?"

Nick's knee jiggled up and down nervously. "Maybe."

"I knew it!"

"But wait." Nick held up a hand. "We don't know *why* the swing was swinging and the corn moved. There has to be some sort of scientific explanation."

"*Pffft.* I don't know about scientific. But the explanation is that there's a ghost." Rebecca grabbed half the comics and dumped them in his lap. "Quick, let's see if there are any more notes."

She took the other half for herself. As they riffled through the pages, she filled Nick in on everything—Dad's supernatural obsession as a kid, the handprint in the abandoned house, hearing whispers and screams in the kitchen, and all the other creepy stuff that had happened that matched her dad's list.

"Uncle Jon says he and my dad weren't allowed near Meadow Winds back then 'cause the people who lived there were mean," Rebecca said. "And get this—the Schmidts own it."

"Huh," Nick said. "You could ask Kelsie if she's seen anything weird."

"No way." Rebecca snorted. "Remember how she made fun of my ghost book?"

Nick flipped through a *Black Panther* comic. "What about your uncle? Maybe he knows something."

Rebecca grimaced. "He acts like my dad was crazy for even believing. He claims nobody has ever seen anything scary around here." She shook the final comic in her stack. Nothing fell out.

"We need to gather more facts," Nick said.

Rebecca's insides fluttered. "You want to help me?"

"Well, I don't think there's actually a ghost," Nick said quickly. "That's what I want to prove."

"And I want to prove there is one." Rebecca chewed her lip. Did it matter if he didn't believe in ghosts? The truth was, she could use help figuring this out. Nick was no Jenna, but it would be awesome to have a ghost-hunting partner again. She nodded. "Okay. The first thing I think we need to do is go back to Meadow Winds."

Nick's face fell. "Really? That place kinda gives me the creeps. Can't we just look around here?"

"No way! It seems like the ghost wants me to go back there. Even my dad thought something was off about that place. It must be the key."

A lion's roar erupted out of nowhere, and she jumped about a mile into the air. Nick sheepishly held up his phone.

"Seriously? That's your ringtone?" Rebecca laughed.

"Hey, my baseball team is the Lions." Nick grinned. He scanned the text, then set his phone down on the table without typing a reply.

"Do you have to go home?" Rebecca asked.

"No," Nick said. "That was Kelsie."

"Kelsie?" Rebecca felt like a bucket of cold water had been dumped over her head. Nick and Kelsie texted each other? "What does she want?"

"She wants to know what time my baseball game is tonight."

"Uh, has she looked outside? It's for sure canceled, the fields are going to be flooded." Rebecca huffed. "Does she come to all your games or something?"

"Usually. I feel kinda bad for her. I don't want to hurt her feelings."

Rebecca bit her tongue. Nick was too nice. Kelsie sure didn't seem to care about other people's feelings. His cell roared a second time.

"This time it's my dad," he said, tapping at his screen. "He says a thunderstorm is coming, so he wants me to get home."

"Oh, okay," Rebecca said. At least it hadn't been Kelsie. "But what about Meadow Winds?"

Nick heaved a sigh. "Okay, I admit I'm curious. I gotta see this handprint you think you saw." He got to his feet.

"That I *did* see," Rebecca corrected.

"Maybe," Nick said doubtfully. "I'll text you when I'm free to meet you there."

"Perfect." They exchanged cell numbers, and then he left.

Instead of going inside, Rebecca reread "Signs of the Ghost." She didn't feel so alone now. Nick was going to help her. Even better, someone else had experienced this ghost. Dad. She carefully smoothed the wrinkles from the envelope, feeling closer to him than ever before. Maybe he'd never solved the mystery of the ghost, but she could try.

As she watched the raindrops begin to fall, Rebecca realized she and Nick hadn't even talked about the comics.

NiNE

"I'm going for a bike ride!" Rebecca called toward Mom's open office door.

She cruised down the driveway on the bike she'd borrowed from Aunt Sylvie. It was two days after the discovery of Dad's "Signs of the Ghost" list. Nick had texted that he had some time before baseball practice to meet her at Meadow Winds. The rain had cleared, no nightmares had tortured her the past couple of nights, and she was ready to face the old house.

As she pedaled past the Schmidt farm, she slowed. Unlike the Graffs' cheerful yellow house, the Schmidts' was painted a dull gray. There weren't any flowers perking up the wide front porch, and most of the shades were drawn. Rebecca felt a tiny twinge of sympathy for Kelsie. No wonder she didn't like her grandpa's house.

Pulling up at a stop sign, Rebecca spied a black pickup about a half mile away coming toward her from the opposite direction. She turned left and continued on. As she neared Meadow Winds, she peeked over her shoulder. The black pickup idled at the stop sign. She squeezed the brakes and decreased her speed. If that truck stayed there much longer, she'd have to ride by the house and double back after it left.

She dawdled along for a couple of minutes, pretending to admire the wildflowers on the side of the road. When she checked again, the truck was gone. She swerved off the road and onto the Meadow Winds driveway, pumping the pedals as fast as she could until she'd rounded the bend and was behind the trees.

There was no sign of Nick yet, but he'd told her it'd take him a while to bike from his house at the edge of town. Rebecca ditched her bike behind an overgrown hedge, walked to the massive oak tree in the front yard, and faced the house.

Unlike Dad, she didn't get the feeling that something was watching her. In fact, the sense of total desolation was back. The door gaped open, exactly as she'd left it after her escape. She studied the bedroom window above it. From where she stood, the glass looked handprint-free. Uh-oh.

A crow dove from the roof and landed on the porch railing. It pecked at the wood, then cawed right at her, a harsh warning to keep away. Rebecca balked. No way was she going past that bird and through the front door without Nick.

To kill time, she circled around to the side of the house she hadn't checked out before. Something jutted up from the waist-high weeds below the dining room window and leaned against the siding. A tall, gray wooden box. Like a coffin. Rebecca caught her breath, then realized it was actually two doors slanting up from the ground.

"Overactive imagination," Rebecca whispered. She needed to stay calm. She moved closer.

Each door had an iron handle. She grabbed one and pulled. To her surprise, the door lifted easily, releasing a surge of cool air and a dank, earthy smell. Wooden stairs led to a dirt floor below.

"Hello?" Rebecca called. As if anyone would be down there. She shook her head.

Nothing moved. She tiptoed down the steps, letting her eyes adjust to the gloom. The cellar was empty, except for the wood shelves lining the dirt walls. In several spots, the ground was messed up, like something had been digging. Mom's warnings about wild animals streaked through her mind.

A long, drawn-out creak came from the house above her. She scanned the undersides of the floorboards over her head. Maybe Nick was up there. She didn't hear any footsteps, though. The silence lengthened. Her pulse beat in her ears. What if the ghost had lured her back to trap her? Any second the cellar door could slam shut.

A shadow crossed the pool of daylight spilling from the open doorway onto the dirt. Rebecca spun around, her heart in her throat. A pair of dirty basketball shoes rested on the top step.

"There you are," Nick said, peering down at her.

"Oh!" Rebecca's hand flew to her chest. "You're here?"

"Well, yeah, you told me to meet you, right?" He came down a couple of steps.

"Right. It's just . . . I heard a noise up there." She pointed at the ceiling. "In the house."

"Oh. Wasn't me," Nick said. He shifted his weight uneasily. "Probably the wind?"

"Probably." Rebecca squared her shoulders. Mom was right; old houses were creaky. "Forget it. Let's go."

Outside, the wind was rising, making the tall grasses ripple and bend. The crow had fled the porch. Rebecca hoped it wasn't hiding inside the house, waiting to attack. She shoved the thought aside and charged through the doorway. "So, the handprint was in the front bedroom." She started up the staircase to the second floor.

"Hold up," Nick said. "I want to look around down here first."

"Oh. Sure."

Rebecca lingered at the foot of the stairs as he wandered through the first floor. Beyond the empty window frames, storm clouds clumped together in the sky. Nick disappeared into the kitchen, and she was alone. Doubts crept into her thoughts. What if the handprint was gone, and he didn't believe it had ever been there? In the living room, the wind whooshed down the chimney like a ghostly train whistle. She hugged her arms to her chest. What was she supposed to find in this abandoned place?

The whistle got louder and morphed into a scream.

"Nick!" Rebecca whipped around.

He was strolling out of the kitchen. "What?"

"Do you hear that?" As soon as she said it, the sound was gone.

"Huh?" Nick's forehead creased with worry. "You keep hearing things. Are you okay? Should we go?" He sounded almost hopeful.

"I . . ." Dad's note to himself flashed across Rebecca's mind. *Be brave.* She took a deep breath. "No. We can't leave yet." She led the way up the stairs.

In the second-floor hallway she paused. "You know, I never looked into these other rooms. We should check them out."

"Fine with me," Nick said.

They went into the back bedroom first. There was nothing interesting in there, only a pile of lumber in a corner near a closet. A side bedroom was completely empty, its window covered by boards. In the bathroom, the tub was cracked in half. The whole place oozed sadness. Rebecca could hardly stand it.

"Okay," Nick said, "I want to see this handprint."

Rebecca realized she was stalling. "Fine."

Together they entered the front bedroom, and she crossed straight to the window. There was a single faint handprint on the glass. She had no idea if it belonged to her or the ghost. Her heart sank.

"I swear there was another handprint there," Rebecca said. "You believe me, don't you?"

Nick shrugged. "I don't know what to say. It's not there now."

Rebecca scrutinized the glass, checking it from different angles. There was no sign of the second handprint. But there was something else. "Wait, what's this?" She pointed to a smudge near the bottom of the pane, one sort of shaped like the letter *V*. "It looks like an arrow pointing down."

Nick squinted. "If you say so."

Rebecca ignored his comment. "It could be a sign." She zeroed in on the window seat. A cupboard and two drawers were built in underneath. She bent over and opened the cupboard doors. One immediately fell off its hinges and banged on the floor.

"Whoops," said Nick.

Rebecca stuck her head inside the space and saw only cobwebs. She turned to the top drawer and yanked its handle. It screeched forward only about an inch. She got on her knees and, after a few more tugs, got it open completely. Nothing was inside.

A trickle of sweat slid down her forehead. The house was beyond stuffy. And what if she was wrong and the smudge wasn't an arrow at all? She tried the bottom drawer. It didn't budge.

"It might be painted shut. Let me try." Nick got on his knees, and Rebecca scooted aside.

He pulled and pushed and wiggled the drawer until it finally broke away from the frame with a sharp crack. Rebecca eagerly peered inside. It was empty. She fell back on her heels, crushed. She'd been so sure the ghost had left her a clue.

"Hey, there could be something in the closet," Nick said encouragingly. He stood and went to investigate.

Rebecca swiped the sweat from her face. So far this visit back to Meadow Winds was a bust. She shoved the drawer in frustration. Instead of gliding straight back under the window seat, it screeched in only halfway and at an angle. She jerked the drawer out as far as she could and tried again. This time the drawer went straight in. But just before it hit the wall, Rebecca heard a slight noise, like the sound of paper crumpling. She checked inside the drawer again. Nothing. But there could be something in the space behind it.

"Nick, help me get this all the way out," she said.

He came to her side, and together they shifted and tugged until the whole drawer thudded to the floor. Rebecca leaned forward. A scrap of paper was wedged against the back wall. She reached in and pulled it out.

"It's an old picture," she said excitedly. "Well, part of one."

She held the left side of a black-and-white photo that had been torn in half. A barefoot girl wearing a high-necked, ruffly dress stood next to a cascade of drooping vines. Beyond some trees behind her, part of a roof and a chimney poked into the sky. But the most striking thing about the photo was the girl's face. She must've been turning her head when the picture was taken, because her face was a featureless white blur beneath a mop of wavy, light hair. Rebecca sucked in a breath, chilled to the bone.

"Okay, that's freaky," Nick said.

Rebecca flipped the photo over. Something had been written on it, but only the ends of four lines remained.

a

d

ra

00

The rest had been torn away.

"I wonder who this is?" Rebecca asked.

"Too bad it's ripped," Nick said.

"This has to be a clue," Rebecca said, her frustration gone and her determination rising. "Right?"

Nick scrunched up his face. "A clue to what?"

"I don't know, but the ghost led me to this house, to this room, to this picture. It obviously wanted me to find it." She leapt to her feet.

"Obviously?" Nick said. "I don't know about that."

"Of course it did!"

Nick's cell roared. He dug it out of his shorts pocket and checked the screen. "Shoot, practice was moved up an hour 'cause it's supposed to rain later. I gotta go."

"You're kidding me," Rebecca said.

"Well, you can stay." He edged toward the hallway, like he was anxious to leave.

Rebecca sure did not want to be in the house alone again. Plus, she'd gotten what she'd come for. "Nah, I should probably get back," she said, faking casualness. She tucked the photo into her back pocket.

As they exited the front door, the same black pickup truck from before sped around the clump of trees and up the driveway. Rebecca backed up, ready to bolt inside, but it was too late. The truck screeched to a halt, horn blaring.

"Uh-oh," muttered Nick.

The driver's-side door swung open, and a stocky old man in ratty overalls and a bright green John Deere feed cap thudded onto the gravel. "What are you kids doing here?" he yelled in a gravelly voice.

Rebecca flinched. Oh boy, they were in trouble. This had to be Kelsie's grandpa.

Nick cleared his throat. "We were riding by, sir—"

"So?" The old man scowled and spat on the grass. Tufts of gray hair poked out over his ears. His face was red and sweaty.

Rebecca plastered on a polite smile. "We're very sorry—"

"Why are kids always sneaking around?" the man said, more to himself than to them. He clenched his fists and took a menacing step forward. "This is private property. Go on home."

They had no choice. Rebecca and Nick scurried to their bikes, and the man plodded toward the crumbling barn.

"Was that old Mr. Schmidt?" Rebecca asked Nick as they pedaled down the driveway.

"Pretty sure," he said. "Man, I thought my grandpa was cranky."

Rebecca laughed, but to her horror, it came out more like a snort. "Oh—" She covered her mouth.

"Nice," Nick said, wrinkling his nose in disgust. For one terrible moment, Rebecca thought he was serious. Then his dimple flashed.

"Nice, yourself!" She swatted at him, hitting his sleeve. Nick clutched his arm, faking extreme pain. She grinned. After the tension of the last hour, it was a relief to joke. They'd reached the end of the driveway. She stopped. "Okay. When can we meet here again?"

"Wow, that old dude didn't scare you at all, did he?" A gleam of admiration shone in Nick's dark eyes.

"No way!" Rebecca said. "We're just getting started."

"I don't know." Nick's eyes clouded over. "Something about this place feels wrong. And I can tell it freaks you out, too."

"It does," Rebecca admitted. She was beginning to realize he couldn't resist a challenge, though, so she took a chance. "But don't you want to find out more? Or prove me wrong?"

Nick snapped the hand brakes on his bike a couple of times, mulling this over. "Okay, fine. Text me. It'll depend on the weather and my baseball schedule." He took off down the road.

Rebecca glanced up the driveway. At first everything was still, then she caught a movement under the trees. Old Mr. Schmidt stood in the shadows, watching her. She reflexively touched her back pocket to check on the photo. It was there, safe and sound. The old man couldn't take that away from her.

TEN

Justin kept Rebecca so busy that afternoon, she didn't have time to worry about old Mr. Schmidt or study the photo. It wasn't until after dinner that she found herself alone and could look at it again.

Uncle Jon was working late, Aunt Sylvie was upstairs reading to Justin, and Mom was on her cell phone in the kitchen. Rebecca wandered onto the front porch and eased into a rocking chair. Maybe when Mom was done with her call they could play a game. At home, the two of them had a game night at least once a week. They'd talked about getting out the Monopoly board a few days ago, and this would be the perfect night.

The dark clouds and drizzling rain gave the world a twilight feel, even though the sun hadn't set. Lightning made the puddles in the yard shimmer.

Rebecca pulled the torn photo out of her pocket and held it in the light spilling from the window behind her. Even though she'd seen it already, the creepy, blurred face still gave her a shock. She plunked the photo facedown on her knee.

The ghost had wanted her to find this picture for a reason. Did that mean the ghost had once been the girl pictured? Rebecca chewed her thumbnail. Kelsie said her family had rented the house to different people over the years, so there was no telling who the girl was. If the Schmidts owned Meadow Winds, though, their family could've lived in it themselves at one point. Maybe the girl in the photo was a Schmidt. Rebecca shuddered. If nasty personalities ran in families, the ghost might be as mean as old Mr. Schmidt and as bratty as Kelsie.

An engine rumbled, and headlights struck her face. Rebecca shielded her eyes and peered down the driveway. Mark Schmidt's rusted truck was splashing toward the house. Her stomach tightened. Uh-oh. Was he coming to yell at her for trespassing at Meadow Winds?

She got up and positioned herself in front of the door, hoping to head him off before he could ring the bell. To her relief, Kelsie wasn't with him. He exited the truck alone, dashed around the puddles, and leapt up the steps. In one hand he carried a plastic bag.

"Hello, Rebecca," Mark said. "You're one of the people I wanted to talk to."

"Oh." Rebecca swallowed. "Okay."

"I'm wondering if you'd like to go to the town pool with Kelsie sometime? We have guest passes."

Phew. "Maybe."

Mark rubbed the back of his neck. "She's been out of sorts lately. Not really sleeping well, I think. Anyway, it would do her some good to hang out with a friend."

A friend? Rebecca almost laughed. Adults were so clueless. Did he not notice Kelsie wanted nothing to do with her? At least he wasn't mentioning Meadow Winds. Old Mr. Schmidt must not have ratted her out. Still, she wasn't going to buy Mark's nice-guy act. He was a Schmidt after all.

Mark held up the bag. "Your mom mentioned her office was a little dim, so I thought I'd surprise her with a desk lamp."

"Great." Rebecca reached for the bag. "I can give it to her."

Mark's eyes crinkled behind his rain-splattered glasses. He held the lamp out of reach. "I'd like to give it to her myself, please."

"Oh. Uh . . ." Rebecca racked her brain for an excuse to keep him out of the house. Behind her the door opened.

"Mark! What a nice surprise," Mom said. "What do you have there?"

"Something for you," he said.

Rebecca had no choice but to shuffle out of the way, clearing Mark's path to the door. He went inside with Mom. Without warning, a waterlogged Jade scampered across the porch, angling to slither into the house as well. Rebecca blocked her with her foot.

"No, Jade. You're supposed to stay outside, remember?" Rebecca snagged a beach towel from a hook inside the front door and closed the door behind Mark. "Let's make you a bed out here."

As she arranged the towel near a flowerpot, she crossed her fingers, hoping Mom wouldn't ask Mark to stay. Aunt Sylvie could join game night and Uncle Jon, too, when he got home. Rebecca was getting used to them. But Mark would ruin it, especially if he and Mom flirted.

The door opened again, and Mom appeared carrying her purse and wearing a raincoat, Mark at her side.

"Wait." Rebecca's face went slack. "You're leaving?"

"We decided to catch a movie, honey," said Mom, beaming.

"B-but . . . remember? We've been talking about having a game night. I thought—"

"Oh, let's do that tomorrow." Mom squeezed Rebecca's hand. "I won't be out late."

"You know, we enjoy a game night, too," Mark said. "Maybe you two and Kelsie and I could play cards sometime."

"What a nice idea," Mom said. Together they went down the steps and toward the driveway.

Resentment burned in Rebecca's chest. She thought of a desperate, last-ditch way to block Mom from leaving. "Also, I wanted to talk about Dad's birthday plans tonight."

To her satisfaction, it worked. Mark continued to the truck, but Mom faltered and stopped. "Oh."

Dad's birthday was coming up in a few weeks, and they always did something special in his honor, like go to a Cubs game or out for Indian food, his favorite. Usually Mom avoided talking about the past, but on Dad's birthday that rule went out the window, and she'd recount all sorts of happy memories. It was always a fantastic day. They both looked forward to it every year.

Mark was holding open the passenger door of his truck, jangling his keys impatiently.

Mom came back up the steps and kissed Rebecca on the cheek. "Well, that's still a few weeks away. We can start planning tomorrow. I promise. Love you, Co-Cap." To Rebecca's astonishment, she turned and left with Mark.

Rebecca kicked at a loose board on the porch floor and watched the headlights from Mark's truck grow smaller and smaller as he reversed down the driveway. Why was this happening? Her mother wasn't supposed to date.

Tears pricked her eyes. None of this was fair. She swiped her wet cheeks with the back of her hand. Her team with Mom had cracked. Stupid Mark. If Mom fell in love with him and they got married, she'd probably force Rebecca to move to Iowa and be sisters with Kelsie. Then mean old Mr. Schmidt would be her step-grandfather, and she'd never see Jenna again.

Talk about a nightmare.

Rebecca sniffled and shuffled toward the front door. The bed she'd made for Jade had been mussed up but was empty. She searched the porch and scanned the yard, but the cat had disappeared.

———

Rebecca did not get a good night's rest. She didn't have any bad dreams, but she'd heard Mom come in around midnight. Which meant she and Mark had done more than just go to a two-hour movie. Gross.

When Rebecca entered the kitchen in the morning, there was a note on the table.

> R, please come see me in my office when you get up. —Mom

Justin crammed scrambled eggs into his mouth while Aunt Sylvie sat with him drinking tea. She nodded at the note. "Hope you're not in trouble," she said jokingly.

Rebecca gave her a tight smile. An order to talk to Mom on a morning she was writing wasn't normal. Usually when she was in the middle of a project, Mom shut herself away all day. What if Mom had gone to the Schmidts' after the movie and heard from old Mr. Schmidt that Rebecca had been trespassing? Maybe she really was in trouble. She gulped a glass of juice, grabbed a golf umbrella from the corner, and went out the back door.

Rebecca ran to the barn as fast as she could. Inside, she leaned the dripping umbrella against a wall. The door to Mom's office was closed. She glanced around for Jade, but there was no sign of her or any other cat. Rain battered the roof and echoed around the cavernous space.

Rebecca hadn't spent much time in the barn since her first night in Iowa. It made her sad to think about Dad playing there as a kid. She hastily made her way to the office door and knocked.

"Come in," called Mom.

Rebecca found her stationed in front of her laptop, a thermos of coffee nearby. A shiny turquoise-blue lamp glowed on a corner of the desk. It did cheer up the place, but Rebecca wrinkled her nose at it anyway.

"Heya, Co-Cap! Please close the door and take a seat." Mom didn't look up from her laptop but pointed out a folding chair wedged in a corner. She wore faded jeans and a long-sleeved T-shirt. The air conditioner droned noisily in the window, but it sure was doing its job. The room was frosty.

Rebecca set up the folding chair near the desk and waited for Mom to stop typing. It always took her a minute to get out of her head and focus on anything other than work.

Finally, Mom swiveled around to face her. "Okay, I'm planning on taking a day off next week so you and I can spend some time alone. Maybe we'll go shopping or to this go-kart place Sylvie told me about. Does that sound good?"

"I guess," Rebecca said, wondering why they had to wait so long to hang out together.

"And last night you mentioned your dad's birthday," Mom continued cheerfully. "You have any idea how you'd like to celebrate?"

Rebecca crossed her arms. "It'll just be the two of us, like normal, right?"

"Well, I thought I might ask Jon to come along, but if you don't want to, that's totally fine."

"I'll think about it," Rebecca grumbled. "I don't know what we should do. There sure aren't any Cubs games or Indian food around here."

"True," Mom said. "We could ask Jon how they used to celebrate here when they were kids."

"I guess." Rebecca focused on her feet and wiggled her toes. Her sneakers were squishy and soaking wet.

There was a moment of silence. Mom tapped her pencil on the desk. "Okay. What's wrong?"

"Nothing." Rebecca kept her head down.

"I can't help if you don't tell me what the problem is."

"I just . . . Fine." Rebecca lifted her chin. "Why are you hanging out with Mark?"

Mom leaned back in her chair, making it squeak. "I enjoy his company."

Rebecca scowled. "What does that mean?"

"Just that. He makes me laugh. I deserve a bit of fun, right? I'm working really hard here." Mom took off her glasses and pinched the bridge of her nose.

"You can have fun with me." Tears stung Rebecca's eyes. She furiously blinked them away.

"Rebecca." Mom tilted her head, her voice going soft. "Of course I can. And I do. But it's okay for me to socialize with other people. That doesn't change anything between the two of us."

"But what about Dad?" Rebecca wrapped her arms tighter around herself.

"Honey, this has nothing to do with your dad. He'll always be a part of our lives. But he's not here."

"Whatever." Rebecca kicked the wastebasket by Mom's desk and it promptly fell over, spilling paper on the floor. She cringed inside. She hadn't meant to kick it that hard, but she couldn't help acting like a baby. Part of her felt out of control and the other part hung back and watched.

"Look." Mom scooped up the paper and shoved it into the wastebasket. "I'm trying to be patient here. But I need you to stop moping. I know you'd rather be at camp, but you have to make the best of this. We're not leaving."

"Fine," Rebecca muttered.

Mom sighed. "Now, I have two jobs for you. One, try to come up with things we can do next week on our day together. And two, talk to Jon about ideas for your dad's birthday. I've got work to do."

And that was it. Mom swiveled back to her computer. She might as well have gone to another planet—within seconds she was tapping at her keyboard and in another world. Rebecca pushed her chair back into the corner.

Stomping through the barn, Rebecca suffered a pin-prick of shame. Mom did a lot for her. As her daughter, she should want Mom to be happy.

On the other hand, wasn't it a mother's job to consider her own kid's feelings?

ELEVEN

The rain dragged on. Which meant Rebecca and Justin were stuck in the house that day instead of going to the pool like she'd hoped. She itched to sneak over to Meadow Winds that afternoon but had no chance. She stayed alert for the ghost, but nothing unusual happened. The hours crept by.

The high point of the day was spotting the postal truck after lunch. Rebecca told Justin to watch her through the window while she ran out to the mailbox. He happily pressed his nose to the glass as she slogged down the mucky driveway to grab the mail. Holding an umbrella in one hand, she gathered the pack of letters and catalogs to her chest and sprinted back to the house as quickly as she could.

As she dumped the mail onto the coffee table, a blue envelope slid to the floor. She ripped into it immediately.

R—okay, no time to write but OMG! A ghost AND a cute boy??? So jealous! J.

That was it? Rebecca slumped against the wall, stung. Her best friend was obviously too busy for her. And doing fine on her own.

During Justin's nap, Rebecca holed up in her room. First, she pulled out the torn photo and studied it until she'd practically committed it to memory. There had to be a clue there she was missing. But the girl in the picture remained suspended in time, revealing nothing new.

Bored, she opened *Heart-Stopping Heartland Hauntings*. The chapter she chose was titled "Chicago's Resurrection Mary." She'd heard the story before, about a girl from the 1930s who'd tried to hitchhike home after a fight with her boyfriend at a dance and was killed by a hit-and-run driver. Rumor had it her ghost haunted the stretch of road where she'd last been seen, near Resurrection Cemetery. The ghost appeared on snowy nights as a girl who needed help on the side of the road. When a driver stopped to give her a ride, she'd get in their car and vanish, leaving the driver terrified. Rebecca read the first paragraph.

Ghosts have various motivations. Sometimes they seek revenge. Sometimes they simply enjoy wreaking havoc on the living. But sometimes they are lost spirits that don't realize they are dead and need to pass on. Thus, they are trapped, reenacting the events around their deaths again and again.

Rebecca slapped the book shut. Resurrection Mary was doing all those things—seeking revenge, wreaking havoc, and reenacting the events around her death. The thought that a spirit could be stuck helplessly wandering between life and death was horrifying. It didn't seem like the ghost haunting her was reenacting its death, though. It must have chosen to linger for another reason. But why? Did it have evil intentions and want to torture the living, like the book said? And how come only she and her dad could sense it?

She rubbed her eyes. A ghost that chose to haunt twelve-year-old kids could definitely be evil. What if it wanted to wreak havoc by making Rebecca do something terrible? If that was the case, she was in way over her head.

To her relief, she heard Justin singing in his room. He was awake. She shut down her thoughts about the ghost and went to get him up.

That night the dream came again.

Rebecca pushed headfirst into shrieking winds. Dark trees thrashed around her, and rain drenched her feverish body. She had to find something—she didn't know what and she didn't know why, but she was sure a terrible disaster would happen if she couldn't. The wind whipped her hair and tore her breath away; her chest ached; she was suffocating. There was a flash and a huge black mass fell at her—

Thunder roared, and Rebecca woke, panting. Shadows filled her room, and rain splattered on the windows. She swiped away a stray curl clinging to her damp cheek and drank in the scene in front of her—the rocking chair in the corner, the quilt folded at the foot of her bed, the dark hallway past her open door.

She was safe. Everything was okay. Kind of.

Except the nightmare was getting scarier and scarier. If real thunder hadn't boomed right outside her window and forced her awake, she'd still be stuck in the dream, for sure.

Rebecca lay still and tried to focus on happy thoughts, like Jenna did so easily. The Cubs were doing great, so that was good. Jenna's dad had bought them tickets to a game in September, which would be totally fun. Uncle Jon had gotten her and Mom guest passes for the town pool, and it'd be nice to go swimming. If the rain ever stopped. She sighed. There she was, right back into her negative thoughts.

A soft scratch came from above. Rebecca's eyes flew to a dark corner of the ceiling near the door.

Silence.

She waited, muscles tense.

Once after hearing sounds like that in the walls at home, they'd caught a mouse in a trap. Mom said mice tried to sneak into houses when the weather turned cold in the fall. It was summer now, but things might be different in the country. Or it could be a squirrel. That would make sense. The roof was probably pretty old and had a hole in it. She'd ask Uncle Jon about it in the morning. She let her eyelids flutter closed.

A long, drawn-out scraping noise shattered the quiet, as if something heavy was sliding slowly across the attic floor. Rebecca jerked upright. That was no animal. Someone was in the attic.

The sound cut off abruptly.

She peered beyond the foot of her bed, past her open door, and into the hall. Nothing stirred. Every other door was closed tight, except the bathroom's, which stood ajar, revealing a night-light shining weakly on the tile floor. None of her family would be in the attic in the middle of the night.

Could it be the ghost?

The second the thought crossed her mind, cold air pressed into Rebecca's skin, sharp as icicles. Down the hall, the attic doorknob began to glow a sickly green. As she watched, terrified, the glow flared and the knob rattled once, twice, three times, finally building into a constantly shaking blur. Rebecca lurched to her knees and pressed back against the headboard. Suddenly the door flew open, and a light blazed down from the attic. The garbled whispering rushed out into the hall and came straight at her. A scream rose in her throat.

The attic door banged shut.

In an instant, everything returned to normal—quiet fell, the air warmed, the doorknob went black.

No one emerged from their room to see what was going on. Everyone had slept through the whole thing. The only proof anything had happened was Rebecca's quivering hands.

TWELVE

Nearing the attic door on her way to breakfast the next morning, Rebecca let her imagination go wild. What if the door blasted open as she went by? What if something reached out and grabbed her, pulled her into the attic, trapped her up there forever? She couldn't go back and hide in her room, though. She shook off the terrible thoughts and scurried toward the stairs.

She made it past the door without a problem.

But Rebecca couldn't shake the memory of the night before. The ghost had been sending her a message. It wanted her to go into the attic. There must be something up there it wanted her to find. The tricky part would be getting past that locked door.

When she got to the kitchen, Uncle Jon, dressed for

work, was rifling through his briefcase at the table. Rebecca got an idea.

"Uh, Uncle Jon? I have a question."

"Yes, Becks?" He didn't look up from shuffling papers. "I'm kind of in a hurry to get to work."

"I'm just wondering if you'd like some help clearing out the attic."

"Absolutely." He snapped his briefcase shut. "Maybe one of these upcoming weekends."

"Or I could start today," Rebecca said, "when Justin is napping."

"No way," Uncle Jon said, sliding his feet into a pair of loafers under the table. "I don't want you going up there alone. Remember, that place is piled high with junk."

"But I'd be careful—"

"Nope. There will be heavy lifting involved. Better wait for me. Also, it's sweltering up there. We'll do it on a cooler day. Gotta run." He grabbed his car keys from the rack by the back door and left.

Rebecca's eyes lingered on the rack. Several sets of keys dangled from it. She waited to hear Uncle Jon's car reverse down the driveway. Mom, Aunt Sylvie, and Justin chattered on the front porch. She was alone. Stepping closer to the key rack, she spotted a single key with a white tag. She held her breath and flipped over the tag. It had one word on it: ATTIC. She exhaled. One problem solved. Now she just needed an opportunity to sneak up there without getting caught.

If she had the guts.

After breakfast, while Aunt Sylvie puttered around the house and Mom wrote in the barn, Rebecca played trucks with Justin in the shade of the maple tree. Whenever her back was to the house, prickles raced along her spine. Up near the roof lurked a window covered by dingy curtains. It stared down at her like a big eye.

The attic and its secrets were up there, waiting.

At eleven o'clock Mom bounded out of the barn. "Hey, guys," she said to Rebecca and Justin. "Let's go to the pool!"

"Yay!" Justin dropped his plastic dump truck and dashed toward the house. "Get my floaties!"

"Rebecca, we'll grab lunch there," said Mom, almost skipping across the yard to the back steps.

Rebecca had never, ever, seen her mother skip before. Something was up. "I thought you were writing all day," she said, standing and brushing stray grass from her shorts.

"Actually, I got a ton done this morning," Mom said over her shoulder. "Then Mark called and suggested the pool. And it's so hot outside. I thought, why not?"

"Oh." Rebecca's stomach dropped. She should've known Mom's peppiness had to do with Mark. "Is Kelsie going, too?"

"Of course." Mom had reached the steps.

That sealed it. Rebecca had no interest in going. A sound echoed through her mind—the slow scrape across the attic floor. This was her chance. She squashed the mixture of jitters and excitement bubbling in her chest and managed to yawn. "Actually, I'm kinda tired," she said. "Do you mind if I stay here?"

"Oh, sweetie." Mom stopped. "I think it would be good for you to see some kids your own age."

"Yeah, it sounds fun, it's just that I didn't sleep great last night. I kinda want to take a nap." Mom looked dubious. Rebecca smiled brightly. "I'll go next time for sure."

"Suit yourself," Mom said. "There are leftovers in the fridge."

Twenty minutes later, everyone was gone. Rebecca paced the upstairs hall, passing the key back and forth between her hands, gathering her nerve. She had no clue what to expect. If the ghost was up there waiting, she'd probably scream and run right back down the stairs. What if going into the attic was a trap? What if—

Rebecca dug her fingernails into her palms. The ghost was obviously trying to communicate with her, and she doubted it would stop. She couldn't ignore it. She needed to be brave, like Dad had pledged to be way back when.

As she turned the key in the lock, the door flew open, as if the sweltering, musty air behind it was desperate to escape. Ahead, a narrow staircase rose into gray half-light. Rebecca put a foot on the first step. The wood groaned. The next step did too, and the next, each of them groaning as she climbed, filling the space with an ominous chorus.

At the top of the stairs, Rebecca stooped so she didn't crack her head on the sloping rafters. She swung around to face the center of the room and teetered, still bent in half.

Uncle Jon had warned her, but nothing could have prepared her for this epic mess.

Heaps of broken furniture, dusty boxes, and sheet-covered shapes loomed in the shadows, covering almost every square inch of floor. The only light came from the low window at the back of the room, a feeble glowing square behind blue-checked curtains.

A bare light bulb dangled from the center of the ceiling. Rebecca picked her way through the chaos, terrified she'd knock over a pile of junk and get buried beneath it. Every step she took sent up a cloud of dust that clogged her nose. Finally, she reached the bulb and pulled the chain. The light that clicked on was so weak, it reached only a few feet. The far corners of the room remained in the shadows.

Rebecca twisted her hands together. The attic seemed to be waiting, watching to see what she'd do. Anything could be hiding behind the piles of forgotten things. If something came at her, there'd be no easy escape. She surveyed the room, wondering if she should get out while she could. At her feet sat a massive black trunk. A dark path cut through the dust on the floor behind it, like the trunk had recently been pushed into the center of the room. Something that big moving across the floor would have made noise—a scraping noise.

"Yes!" she hissed. Curiosity overcame her jitters. This must be where she was supposed to start.

She dropped to her knees, hoping she didn't need to find another key. To her relief, the trunk wasn't locked. It took all her strength to lift the lid.

The first thing she saw was a stack of old-fashioned clothes. Rebecca sifted through them eagerly, discovering long dresses with rows of tiny pearl buttons, a couple of embroidered skirts, some frilly blouses. A flat rectangular box held a mass of tissue paper and a tiny gown of white lace, probably for a baby's christening. At the bottom of the stack lay a beautiful black-velvet cloak with a pin made of peacock feathers. The clothes seemed like movie costumes, not anything real people had actually worn. As cool as they were, though, they didn't give Rebecca any information about the ghost.

Underneath the clothes was a collection of musty Sears catalogs. Remembering how Dad's note had been tucked into a comic, Rebecca leafed through them until she found a large manilla envelope. She eagerly opened it and tilted it to one side. A thick piece of paper and some black-and-white photos tumbled into her hand. She sat, crossing her legs, and settled in.

The paper was a marriage certificate for William Joseph Foxx and Eleanor Katherine Reimers dated October 14, 1887. Wow. According to Uncle Jon, William Foxx had built the house she was currently sitting in. Rebecca ran her fingers over the thick paper. It was strange to hold something that old. She carefully set it aside and turned to the photos.

The first was a black-and-white portrait of a chubby-cheeked baby girl propped on a spindly chair. She wore a puffy-sleeved dress, a big bow in her wispy hair, and an expression so serious it was almost funny. But when Rebecca looked closer, she was blindsided.

The Graff family eyes were staring right at her.

Hands trembling, Rebecca turned over the photo. Two lines were written on the back. Straining to remember her third-grade cursive lessons, she made out the words.

Clara Caroline Foxx
On her first birthday, May 14, 1889.

Rebecca bit her lip. Hadn't Uncle Jon said something about a relative named Caroline from way back when? This baby could be the daughter of William and Eleanor. She studied the photo. She knew about heredity and stuff, but it was still weird seeing someone from over a hundred years ago who looked like her. This baby had been part of her family. Her great-something-grandmother. In spite of the stifling heat in the attic, she shivered.

She put the portrait atop the marriage certificate and picked up the next photo. In it four people in fancy clothes posed stiffly on a front porch—definitely the same porch that was two flights down from her. A gloomy, bald old man and a bent, dour old woman flanked a somber young couple. Rebecca shook her head. It was weird how no one looked happy in old pictures. The young man was broad-shouldered with a dark mustache, and the young woman held a bouquet of flowers and had the family eyes. She checked the back of the photo.

Clara Foxx and Thomas Graff, married June 1, 1907.
With William Foxx and Gertrude Foxx.

Wow, Clara, all grown up. Rebecca gawked at the picture and did the math. Clara was only nineteen years old on her wedding day. People sure got married young back then. And Thomas Graff was her husband. These details lined up with the family history Uncle Jon had mentioned. But who was this stern-faced Gertrude, and where was Clara's mother, Eleanor? The picture gave her no answers.

The other photos were snapshots taken outside. One showed a shaggy dog standing in the snow, one an old-timey car parked near a barn, one a horse grazing in a field. The final photo was of a young girl perched on a man's shoulders near a lush cornfield. They both had light hair and broad smiles. The girl had the family eyes, though the man didn't. The inscription on the back read:

Clara and William. August 1899.

Rebecca inspected the photo thoughtfully. So, this was Clara with her dad when she was little. William had a lot more hair and looked much happier in this picture than he did in the one from Clara's wedding. Life probably hadn't been easy back then.

It struck her that something more than Clara's eyes

seemed familiar: the shade of her hair and the way it floated in waves and curls around her head. An image she'd memorized popped into her mind. Her hand flew to her mouth.

Clara was the same girl from the photo she'd found at Meadow Winds. In this picture her face wasn't blurred and scary, but her hair told the same story. And the *ra* on that photo could've been the end of the name *Clara*. This meant she—Rebecca—could be related to the ghost. But why would a picture of Clara be stuck behind a drawer at Meadow Winds? And if the Schmidts were connected somehow, had they done something to Clara?

She needed more information.

Rebecca dug into the trunk with new energy. There were a ton of old books, a lot of classics like *Little Women* and *A Christmas Carol*. All had Clara's name written on the inside cover. She leafed through them each, finding nothing.

At the very bottom of the trunk was one last book, *The Tales of Edgar Allan Poe*. When Rebecca picked it up, the book naturally fell open to a section in the middle. A rectangular hole had been cut into a large chunk of pages. Nestled inside was a folded packet of paper tied with a baby-blue ribbon. She gingerly lifted the fragile bundle, hoping it didn't disintegrate in her hands. Faint ink showed through the back of the paper. She broke out in a new layer of sweat.

Needing more light and some air, Rebecca took her new discovery to the window. She pushed aside the ratty curtains and grabbed the sash. Luckily the window opened. A sticky breeze drifted inside. Beyond the backyard and cornfield, parts of the creek, the thicket of trees, and a sliver of Meadow Winds' roof were visible. A hawk soared noiselessly in the sky. Clouds were once again building on the horizon.

She couldn't wait another second to find out what was in the packet. Rebecca untied the ribbon and unfolded the papers. The left edge of each was tattered, as if it had been torn out of a book. Spidery writing in faded black ink slanted across the first page. It read:

> September 15, 1900
> Dear Diary,
>
> I am sad. I am angry. I am scared.
> Father says I am to write my thoughts in this notebook. He doesn't like talking about emotions or the past. That's all well and good, but I need someone to talk to.
> I suppose you're all I've got.
>
> Yours, Clara

Rebecca swallowed. Holy cow. She'd found pages from Clara's diary. She reread the date. The photo of Clara as a one-year-old was from 1889, which meant in 1900 she would've been twelve—the same age Rebecca was now. Wow. These were Clara's private thoughts. She'd been a real person with real emotions, not just a face in some old photographs. Rebecca shifted to the next page.

September 20, 1900
Dear Diary,

Last night there was a terrible thunderstorm. I don't believe it has rained since July, when it rained so very much and things got so awful. Father always said too much rain is as bad as too little. He was right.

Today I went to the creek and sat under the willow. When I got there, the wind whispered in the branches and rustled the leaves. I knew I was not alone.

Father just returned home. No time to write more.

Yours, Clara

Rebecca blinked. What did that mean—Clara knew she was not alone? It almost sounded like she'd felt the presence of a ghost. Maybe the same ghost stalking her now had haunted Clara way back then. She blew a wisp of hair out of her eyes, her thoughts whirling. She read on.

October 14, 1900
Dear Diary,

Another storm last night. Will I ever be able to sleep through one again?

Father speaks of selling the house, building a new one, and starting fresh. That makes me angry. I do not want to leave.

Uncle Henrich and his new wife are coming from Germany to stay awhile. I made a secret spot in my closet to hide you away and keep you safe. No one will ever find you.

Yours, Clara

Rebecca blew out a breath. Obviously Clara had never moved away. But why did her dad want a fresh start? There was only one more page. Some of the words were just bumpy, inky smudges, but she could make out most of them.

October 26, 1900
Dear Diary,

— —uld be so different if Mother were alive. I
wish I'd known her.

Rebecca's grip tightened on the paper. So, Clara's
mom had died when she was little. She'd grown up with
one parent gone, too. A swell of compassion flowed
through her.

Life isn't fair. That makes me so angry.
Father tells me not to dwell on the past, but
to look forward, as he do — — trying. Today
I went to the willow, buried — — — — —, and
marked the sp— — —symbol. Because that is
wher— — —box belongs, forever and ever. It
shouldn't be anywhe— —lse.

You— —ra
P.— —urse on any— — disturbs it!

Rebecca frowned. What was this stuff about burying
a box and a symbol? And that P.S. at the bottom? She
ran through possible words ending in *urse*. Nurse, purse,
curse. That's probably what it was. "A curse on anyone
who disturbs it."

The threat gave Rebecca the creeps. The curtains wafted around her. The world stood by, eerily calm.

"What happened to you back then, Clara?" Rebecca whispered.

Immediately the temperature in the attic nosedived. A violent wind whipped past her and out the window, rattling the glass and sucking the curtains outside the frame. She pushed to her knees, the letters dropping from her hands and then scattering across the floor. Below, a ripple tore through the cornfield—like the wind from the attic was racing directly to Meadow Winds. A glint of sunlight hit the creek and sent a blinding flash into her eyes. A faint scream echoed in the air, joined by another. Rebecca struggled to her feet.

All at once everything stopped. The curtains went limp. The screams died. The heat blasted back in full force. Rebecca sank to the floor, the sound of her ragged breath filling the attic.

That had been a definite signal. The ghost—whoever it had once been—wanted her to go back to Meadow Winds. Despite what Mom had said, despite any dangers, she had to keep digging for answers.

THiRTEEN

Though she was still shaking from her latest encounter with the ghost, Rebecca made herself take another quick look through the trunk, in case she'd missed any clues. She even checked the pockets in the old clothes but didn't find a thing. Outside the sun had disappeared and the sky threatened rain. Her family could come home at any second, and she did not want to get caught where she shouldn't be. After grabbing the diary pages and the photos, Rebecca scooted down the stairs, locked the attic door, and returned the key to its hook.

In her room she texted Nick.

Call me ASAP. Found new info!!!!

She stashed the diary pages and photos under a pile of T-shirts in her dresser drawer.

It wasn't long before her family came back from the pool. Rebecca was waiting on the porch, innocently leafing through a magazine.

"Well, it was fun while it lasted." Aunt Sylvie held on to a whining Justin's hand and nudged him into the house.

Mom lagged behind, carrying the diaper bag and wet towels. "You didn't miss much, Co-Cap. Kelsie seemed bummed you weren't there, though."

"Really?" Rebecca didn't believe that for a second.

"Yes. And good news—Mark is making his famous barbecued chicken tonight and invited us over for dinner."

Rebecca cringed. Why did Mom have to see him again? How could she be so happy about a guy who wasn't Dad? "Us, meaning just you and me?"

"Yup." Mom was already inside the house.

Rebecca's stomach clenched nervously. "What about Mark's dad?" she called.

"Actually, he has other plans. Please be ready at six."

Rebecca relaxed a teensy bit. At least she wouldn't have to deal with mean old Mr. Schmidt.

Before Mom rang the doorbell at the Schmidts', she placed her hand on Rebecca's shoulder. "Okay. I get the feeling you're not a huge fan of Kelsie's. Remember, we're guests here, though, so be polite."

"I know," Rebecca said, wriggling away.

Mom rang the bell.

Kelsie answered so quickly she must've been waiting on the other side of the door. Rebecca wondered with a stab of guilt if she'd overheard them.

"Come in," Kelsie said unenthusiastically. Her bubblegum-pink T-shirt brought out the dark circles under her eyes. Her dad was right—it definitely looked like she hadn't been sleeping well.

"Hi there," Mom said, holding out a cake platter. "We brought dessert. Hope you like chocolate."

"It's okay, I guess," Kelsie said. She grudgingly took the platter.

Rebecca bit the inside of her cheek. Kelsie couldn't even pretend to like chocolate, much less say thanks. She had to be the rudest person ever.

The Schmidts' hallway decor consisted of ancient shag carpet and foil-striped wallpaper. Rebecca couldn't quite identify the stale smell wafting around, but she sure didn't like it. Mark walked toward them through a wood-paneled dining room, wiping his hands on an apron printed with the words WORLD'S BEST CHEF.

"Hi, Chrissy!" He swooped in and gave Mom a kiss on the cheek. She blushed.

Rebecca winced. *Chrissy?* She got a noseful of his overpowering cologne and stifled a sneeze.

"Glad you two could make it," Mark continued. "Chrissy, the grill is out back, come with me. Kel-Kel, maybe Rebecca would like to see your room."

"Uh . . ." Kelsie stared at the cake platter, her face a blank mask. "I should put this away."

"I got it," Mark said, sweeping it out of her hands.

Kelsie trudged toward the staircase, but Rebecca's feet stayed glued in place. Mark acted like this was a preschool playdate and he needed to arrange an activity for them.

"Go on, Co-Cap," Mom said, shooting her a warning look. As Rebecca shuffled away, Mom and Mark began chatting and laughing, their voices growing fainter as they headed to the kitchen.

Kelsie was now in a big hurry, taking the stairs two at a time. When Rebecca reached the second floor, the only reason she guessed which bedroom was Kelsie's was by the sound of drawers opening and closing. She entered a tiny room just as Kelsie kicked some mud-splattered sneakers under the bed. It was clear she was trying to hide them.

"I don't like people in my business," Kelsie grumbled. "I don't know what I'm supposed to show you, but here it is."

Rebecca assessed the room. A twin bed covered by a frayed lilac comforter lined one wall. There was a chipped white dresser, a mostly empty bookcase, and a window with a dingy roller shade.

"It's nice," Rebecca said politely.

"Whatever." Kelsie snatched a flashlight from the nightstand and shoved it into a drawer. "My mom is setting up a room for me in L.A. that's going to be awesome. It has a view of the Hollywood Hills."

"That's cool," Rebecca said. An arrangement of beach-scene snapshots covered the wall over the bed. "Did you take those pictures?"

"My mom did."

"What beach is it?"

"I don't know, some place in California." Kelsie flopped down onto the bed, leaving Rebecca standing awkwardly in the doorway. Rebecca cast her eyes around the room, trying to find something else to comment on. On the dresser there was an arrowhead collection—two dozen of them spaced so evenly it could've been a museum display.

"These are cool," said Rebecca, stepping closer to get a better look.

"Don't touch." Kelsie shot from the bed and pushed past her, blocking her way.

"Okay." Rebecca backed up. "Where'd you get those?"

"I found them myself around here," Kelsie said. Rebecca wondered if that was the reason for Kelsie's muddy shoes and dirty fingernails. "I think they could be worth a ton of money."

"Maybe," said Rebecca.

The conversation stalled. They eyed each other. Kelsie's fingers wrapped around the gold chain visible above the neck of her T-shirt. There was a bump under the fabric near her collarbone, like the chain held a medallion or charm.

"What's on your necklace?" Rebecca asked.

Kelsie's eyes narrowed. "A locket."

"Can I see it?"

"No."

"Why do you always tuck it under your shirt?" Rebecca asked.

A strange expression flitted across Kelsie's face, then disappeared. "My mom gave it to me. It upsets my dad to see it. It reminds him of her."

"Oh." Rebecca had no clue what to say to that. This

she understood. She almost felt sorry for Kelsie. Sometimes Mom got all quiet when someone mentioned Dad. Rebecca had learned to not bring him up too much. Except on Dad's birthday—that day she could talk as much as she wanted to about him, and Mom was happy to. That day was a celebration. She twirled a curl around her finger and hoped dinner would be ready soon.

"You know, you ask a lot of questions," Kelsie said.

"Yeah, well, I'm just trying to talk to you," Rebecca answered.

"I'm not really sure why you guys are here."

At least Kelsie was honest. "Me neither," Rebecca said.

"I mean, no offense, but my mom is way prettier than yours. And smarter." Kelsie planted her hands on her hips. "I'm sorry you don't have a dad, but you're not getting mine, believe me."

"I don't want your dad," Rebecca huffed.

"Sure you do." Kelsie rolled her eyes. "And it's totally obvious your mom is hunting for a new husband."

Anger, hot and electric, boiled up in Rebecca. "That's not true!"

"Girls?" Mark's voice floated up from the first floor. "Will you please come set the table?"

Kelsie barged out of the room. Rebecca's momentary drop of sympathy for her evaporated.

The rain had stopped, but it was so humid outside they ate in the dining room, where an air-conditioning unit buzzed from the window. As much as Rebecca hated to give Mark any credit, his barbecued chicken was delicious. Between that, the homemade potato salad, and cucumbers straight from the garden, she ate her fill.

Kelsie acted much nicer around her dad. She'd probably gotten a lecture about being polite, too. Overall, dinner wasn't too bad.

But as Rebecca took her first bite of chocolate cake, heavy footsteps thumped through the back door and into the kitchen. She choked down her mouthful. Old Mr. Schmidt must be home. There was a chance Mom was going to find out she'd gone back to Meadow Winds after all.

"Dad?" called Mark. "Your timing is impeccable. We just started dessert."

He winked at Rebecca. She forced a smile.

"What? Oh." Mr. Schmidt shuffled into the dining room. Without a hat, his head was completely bald except for the clump of gray hair over each ear. He'd exchanged his overalls for baggy khaki pants and a golf shirt, but he was definitely the same person who'd yelled at Rebecca at Meadow Winds. "Evening." He nodded at Mom and studied Rebecca for a moment, his eyes blank. Then they sparked with recognition.

Rebecca picked up her water glass and took a shaky sip.

"Hi, Grandpa," Kelsie bounced out of her seat and hugged the old man. He gave her hand a distracted pat, and she smirked at Rebecca, like he was bowing at her feet or something. As if Rebecca wanted to steal her grandpa away, too. Ha! If Kelsie only knew.

"Dad," Mark said, "this is Christine's daughter, Rebecca. Rebecca, this is my father."

"Oh yes. Now I see. You're a Graff child." Mr. Schmidt's wiry gray eyebrows lowered. "I remember Ben."

Rebecca carefully placed her glass on the table. The thought that Mr. Schmidt might've known Dad had not occurred to her at all. "You knew my dad?"

"I did." The old man pulled out a chair at the end of the table and sat heavily.

Kelsie flounced back to her place.

"Mr. Schmidt, would you like some dessert?" Mom asked, holding a knife over the cake.

"Thank you, I would." He leveled his watery blue eyes at Rebecca. "Your father was always getting into some thing or another."

Rebecca twisted her fingers in her lap. He was going to tell on her for sure.

Mom laughed. "That sounds like Ben."

Mr. Schmidt grimaced. "*My* son was made to do his share of the work."

Mark sighed. "Dad, to be fair, Ben and Jon were guests when they came here. And little kids. Sure, I was working then, but I was a teenager."

"Wait," Rebecca said. "You knew my dad, too?"

"Well, yeah, I saw him around." Mark aimed a smile at Mom, who was cutting the cake. She smiled back. Obviously this was no surprise to her. Rebecca was shocked. The Schmidts knew more about the Graffs than she did.

"Rebecca isn't very familiar with her dad's side of the family," Mom said, reading her mind. She handed Mr. Schmidt a plate with a slice of cake.

"I know a ton about mine." Kelsie licked frosting from her fingers. "My mother's family came over on the *Mayflower*."

"I think your mom's stretching the truth on that one, Kelsie," Mark said. "So, Dad, you've known the Graff family a long time. Any interesting history you can share with Rebecca?"

This was another new angle for Rebecca. She leaned forward.

The old man's jaw moved side to side as he finished

chewing. "When I was a boy, a widow lived in what's now your uncle's house. She and her son's family. We called her Grandma Graff."

"What was her first name?" Rebecca asked eagerly.

"Clara, I believe. She passed on not long after we moved in."

Old Mr. Schmidt had known Clara! Rebecca slapped a palm on the table. "How did she die?" She'd read in *Heart-Stopping Heartland Hauntings* that a violent death could cause a spirit to linger in the world of the living. Whatever had happened to Clara might give Rebecca some insight into the ghost.

She realized with a shock that everyone was staring at her.

"Honey, that's an odd question," Mom said.

"Sure is," said Mr. Schmidt.

Kelsie snorted. "I get it. Rebecca is into ghosts, Grandpa. I mean, I used to like that stuff, too. When I was little."

Mark's face lit up. "Actually, I find the idea of ghosts fascinating."

Rebecca gave him the side-eye. Finally someone else showed interest in the supernatural, and it had to be Mark?

"Ghosts are nonsense," Mr. Schmidt said. "However,

I do know how Mrs. Graff died. I remember, her first great-grandchild was about to be born and she was thrilled, so my mother said." He wiped his mouth with a napkin. "But Mrs. Graff didn't get to meet the baby. She went to bed a few nights before he was born and never woke up again."

Silence fell on the table.

Rebecca wilted. It was good that Clara hadn't been shot or pushed off a bridge or anything. But it was too bad she hadn't lived long enough to meet her great-grandson. "That's sad," she murmured.

"That's life," said Mr. Schmidt. "People die. That's a good way to go, in your sleep when you're old."

Mom picked up a spoon and stirred her iced tea, the ice cubes clinking noisily against the glass. Her eyes glazed over. Rebecca's stomach tightened. She could tell Mom was thinking about Dad and getting all gloomy.

Mr. Schmidt jutted his chin at Rebecca. "You're a very curious young lady. Much like your father. He used to go where he wasn't supposed to, as well." Her stomach dropped. "Here's another fact you may be interested in. A member of your family built that house I caught you sneaking around in today."

His words hung in the air for a moment. Then everyone started talking at once.

"Who?" said Rebecca.

"What?" said Mom.

"Where?" said Mark.

"Huh?" said Kelsie.

The old man folded his hands across his belly and surveyed the faces around him. He clearly enjoyed the chaos he'd unleashed. "Yes. Grandma Graff's father built Meadow Winds in 1885. A Mr. William Foxx."

Kelsie's mouth opened and closed like a fish, like she couldn't figure out what to say.

Rebecca leaned forward. "Do you know why they sold the house? Did your family buy it from them?" She needed some answers before Mom started in on her.

"No and no," said Mr. Schmidt. "The Foxxes had sold it to another family years before we purchased it."

"Wait a minute," Mom said, holding her hand up. "Rebecca Anne, I'm disappointed in you. I specifically told you not—"

"Mom, Nick and I were just riding by and—"

"You were with Nick?" Kelsie's face turned red.

Mom pointed a finger at Rebecca. "We'll talk about this later, young lady."

"I'd prefer no one go around that house," said Mr. Schmidt. "Why are kids always sneaking around?" This time he glared at Kelsie. Her eyes darted nervously.

Hmmm. Rebecca made a mental note. Looked like she and Kelsie had one thing in common—they liked to explore.

"Dad, it'll be gone in a couple of weeks, so it won't be a problem much longer," said Mark.

"What?" Kelsie's voice squeaked. "I thought you weren't tearing it down until September."

"Nope, got the permits all figured out," said Mr. Schmidt gruffly.

"But . . ." New information was flying around the table so quickly, Rebecca felt light-headed. "You can't tear it down. That's my family's history."

"They can do whatever they want with it, Rebecca," Mom said. "It's their property."

Mr. Schmidt pushed back from the table. "I'm headed upstairs."

"Tell you what." Mark stood and stretched his arms. "If everyone is finished, let's play cards."

"That sounds like a good idea," said Mom.

As Mr. Schmidt clomped out of the room and everyone else got up, Rebecca remained planted in her seat, her mind spinning like a fastball. This new info changed everything. If William Foxx had built Meadow Winds, then Clara must've lived there. Now it made sense why her photo was lodged under the window seat. That bedroom might even have belonged to her.

Rebecca made a promise right then and there to herself, to Dad, and to the ghost. She wouldn't just *try* to figure out the mystery of the ghost; she *would* figure it out. She had to, for the sake of her family. And she had to do it soon, before Meadow Winds was destroyed.

FOURTEEN

On the drive back from the Schmidts', while Mom lectured about following rules, Rebecca hardly paid attention. Instead she stared out into the night, still trying to digest what she'd learned at dinner.

"Co-Cap?" Mom rapped on the dashboard. "Rebecca!"

Rebecca blinked. "Sorry, what?"

"Promise me you won't go back to Meadow Winds," Mom said, using her I'm-disappointed-in-you tone.

Rebecca hated lying, but no way could she stay away from that house. She crossed her fingers under the empty cake platter she held on her lap. "I promise."

Mom gave her a sidelong glance. "Is that book Jenna gave you putting ideas in your head about haunted houses or something?"

"No." Rebecca slouched in the seat. The cornfield

outside the window was darker than dark. Anything could hide in there.

"If it is, maybe I should take it away from you."

"I said it wasn't!" Rebecca said. "If Dad were alive, he wouldn't be like this. He'd understand."

"Understand what?" Mom said sharply.

"You know—about ghosts!"

"Honey, he may have believed in ghosts as a kid, but he didn't as an adult."

"How do you know?"

"Because I knew him, okay?" Mom gripped the steering wheel tighter. "Listen, I don't know why we're even discussing this. Stay away from that house."

She pulled the car up next to Uncle Jon's. Rebecca exited before Mom had even turned off the engine. For once the night sky wasn't covered with clouds, but she wasn't in the mood to appreciate the fantastic number of stars, a sight she couldn't get at home. She stormed into the house.

"Hi, Becks!" Uncle Jon stood in the kitchen holding a carton of ice cream. "How was dinner?"

"Interesting, actually." Rebecca marched straight toward him.

"Do tell." He set the carton on the counter, opened a cupboard, and retrieved a bowl. "Sylvie is having a craving. Want some ice cream?"

"No, thank you." Rebecca plopped the cake platter into the sink. Behind her, Mom entered the house and headed to the second floor. "Uncle Jon, did you know William Foxx built Meadow Winds?"

"You don't say." He rested the ice cream scoop in the bowl and leaned against the counter. "Who told you that?"

"Old Mr.— Kelsie's grandpa."

"Fascinating. Well, he'd know since he owns the place now and probably has all of the paperwork." He rubbed his chin. "Did he say what year?"

"Yeah, 1880-something."

"Huh. This house was built in 1901, so William Foxx must've lived there before he moved here. I do know that our family at one point owned a ton of farmland around here." He began scooping ice cream into the bowl.

Rebecca wrapped a curl around her finger, thinking. Clara's diary was dated 1900, so her dad probably did move them out of Meadow Winds after she'd written that he'd wanted to. But they didn't move very far. "So you didn't know about this?"

"Nope," Uncle Jon said. "At least I don't remember ever hearing about it. I was here, though."

"I wonder if my dad knew," Rebecca said.

Uncle Jon shook his head. "I doubt it. He was fascinated

by Meadow Winds, though. He always wanted to explore over there, but as I told you, we weren't allowed. It was run-down even then and looked kinda spooky, which probably intrigued him." He finished scooping the ice cream and gazed thoughtfully out the kitchen window. "Come to think of it, I remember one time we were fishing at the creek . . . and a big storm was brewing. The sky was getting dark, so we had to get home. But Ben was acting weird. He kept pacing the creek bank, staring toward Meadow Winds, asking me if I felt the cold. If I felt the sad ghost. Something like that. Huh." Uncle John snapped the ice cream lid back in place and carried the carton to the freezer.

"Wait, but did you? Feel the sad ghost?"

Uncle Jon laughed. "No, but he was my big brother, you know, so I think I pretended I did." He shrugged. "I told you Ben had a big imagination. Although maybe he was just trying to scare me. It's hard to recall."

"Jon?" Aunt Sylvie's voice floated from the second floor to the kitchen. "You're not eating my ice cream, are you?"

"Oops! Gotta fulfill my duties!" Uncle Jon grabbed the bowl of ice cream from the counter and patted Rebecca's shoulder. "Good night, Becks." He rushed out of the room.

Rebecca trailed behind him slowly. If Uncle Jon's memory was right, Dad had thought the ghost was sad, which was strange. To her, the ghost came off as desperate, almost angry. Scary, too. She chewed her thumbnail, wishing for the umpteenth time she could talk to Dad. Even if he'd stopped believing in ghosts, like Mom claimed he had, he would listen. She absolutely knew it.

When Rebecca got to her room, she retrieved her phone from her drawer—Mom had insisted she not bring it to dinner—and checked for a text from Nick. He'd finally answered.

New clues? Hope they lead to a SCIENTIFIC explanation lol

BTW going to visit my bros w my dad, back in 2 days

Seriously? Rebecca tossed her phone on the bed. Right when she really needed his help, he was leaving. It wasn't Nick's fault, but still. Waiting was the worst. Even though it was getting late, she texted him the latest bombshell, that Meadow Winds had been built by her family. The rest was just too much to put into a text. If only she could talk to Jenna!

She could at least send her a letter. Rebecca grabbed a pad of paper from her nightstand and started writing. She explained all the new details—Dad's "Signs of the Ghost," the torn photo, the trunk in the attic, and that her own family had built Meadow Winds. By the time she finished, she was wiped out. A lot had happened that day. She got into her pj's, crawled into bed, and opened *Heart-Stopping Heartland Hauntings*.

Tonight's story was called "The Haunted Vessels of Lake Superior" and told of an 1850s captain whose ship capsized in a terrible November storm, killing everyone aboard. From then on, when weather conditions were similar, a phantom ship would pull aside boats on the lake, and the captain's terrifying ghost would moan, "Go back!" Those who followed its advice survived. Many did not, resulting in dozens of November shipwrecks since 1850.

The story began:

There is a phrase "history repeats itself." It is said some ghosts appear as warnings, omens of impending tragedies. The living should pay heed.

A shiver skittered down Rebecca's spine.

There was a knock on her door.

"Come in," Rebecca said, raising her guard. She shoved her book under the quilt.

Mom opened the door. She was wearing her robe and glasses. "Hi, sweetie. I just wanted to say good night."

"Okay. Good night."

Mom lingered in the doorway. "It's just . . . not productive to talk about your dad and ghosts."

"Okay," Rebecca said shortly.

"I don't want another call from the police or for you to

get hurt in a building that is set to be demolished, you know?" Mom toyed with the belt of her robe. "I'm only trying to keep you safe."

Rebecca softened. "I know."

"I'm sorry we argued before."

"Me too."

"I love you."

"I love you too, Mom."

Mom retreated into the hall and closed the door. Rebecca tossed the book to the floor and wiggled farther under the covers. She felt a little guilty about planning to go back to Meadow Winds, but she didn't want her mom to worry. It struck her again how much she and Clara had in common. Clara's dad hadn't been able to deal with his daughter's feelings, either, just like Mom couldn't deal with hers. He'd given Clara a diary and told her to stop talking about them.

Rebecca could relate, for sure. Poor Clara. That grumpy-looking Gertrude must have been her stepmother.

She rolled over. Why couldn't parents wait to die until their kids were all grown up?

FIFTEEN

"So you think Clara is the ghost?" Nick asked Rebecca as they pushed their bikes behind the abandoned farmhouse.

He'd gotten back to town and Rebecca was filling him in on all that had been happening. She'd had to wait an agonizing three whole days after dinner with the Schmidts for a chance to sneak over to Meadow Winds. A half hour before, from her bedroom window, she had spotted old Mr. Schmidt get on his tractor, and Kelsie and Mark driving toward town in the truck. Mom was writing, Uncle Jon was at work, and Aunt Sylvie had taken Justin to the dentist. Rebecca had immediately texted Nick, and he'd agreed to meet her at Meadow Winds for a bit before his baseball game. They were very careful to make sure no one saw where they went.

"Could be. Or it might be that Clara was haunted by

the ghost, too." Rebecca plunked her bike in the weeds. "Either way, she lived in this house and we found her photo here. It was her trunk that moved. As soon as I said her name in the attic the air got all freaky again—"

"And you saw a wind go through the corn." Nick raised an eyebrow and dropped his bike next to hers.

"I know, I know." Rebecca had to admit that that part sounded weird out loud. "But let me finish. You know how there were only a few diary pages? Clara wrote that she made a secret place in her closet to hide the diary. So I'm hoping the rest might be in there. And maybe that's what the ghost wants us to find."

"You think it will still be there after a hundred years?" Nick sounded doubtful.

"I don't know. But I've gotta try."

They entered the house through the kitchen and continued straight to the second floor. At the top of the stairs, Rebecca stopped short. Something had changed. The hall seemed dimmer than she remembered. The doors to three rooms stood open, but the fourth, the one at the back of the house, was closed.

"Wasn't that door open the last time we were here?" she asked.

"Huh?" Nick halted, too. "I think so. Maybe the wind shut it."

They gawked at the closed door. The house was way too quiet, like it was holding its breath and listening. Rebecca's palms grew clammy. She understood now what her dad meant when he said he felt like something was watching him at Meadow Winds.

A clatter echoed behind the door. Rebecca and Nick locked eyes. She gathered all her courage and lunged at the doorknob.

"What are you doing?" Nick yelled.

Rebecca flung open the door and ducked to one side. In the dim room, three small gray forms shot across the floor. She burst into nervous laughter. "Just some mice."

"Oh, man," Nick said sheepishly. He pointed to the stack of boards in the corner. "They probably have a nest in there."

"Yup," Rebecca said. Sure enough, one of the stacked boards had fallen and rested by itself on the floor. Nothing else had been disturbed. She clapped her hands together. "Okay, let's do this thing."

She led the way into the front bedroom. One handprint remained on the window, but the arrow-like smudge was gone. She stepped into the tiny closet. There was no space for Nick, so he stayed behind.

"I'll keep watch," he said. "The mice could attack."

"Ha," Rebecca said. She went to work. First she

inspected the walls and pressed any cracks in the plaster, searching for a hidden door. No luck. Then she knelt and slid her fingertips along the cracks between the floorboards to test if any of them were loose. Nope. Finally, she studied the ceiling. It looked normal. Walls, floor, ceiling—nothing. Three strikes. She was out.

"I can't find anything," Rebecca said, beyond disappointed. "Either Clara was really tricky, or this is the wrong bedroom. Or . . ." Her gaze drifted to a low corner of the closet. Where the long rear wall met the short side wall, there was a slight, crooked gap. She crawled forward and managed to ease her fingernails inside. The shorter baseboard dropped open with a slap. "Aha!"

"What?" Nick crowded into the closet.

Behind the baseboard was a shallow space, large enough to hide a small notebook. But it was empty.

Rebecca's excitement dissolved. "Shoot." She should've known it wouldn't be this easy.

Nick squatted next to her. "Wait a minute." He stuck his hand into the space and pointed at a mark carved into the wall. "C. F.," he said. "Clara Foxx. So at least that part of the diary checks out."

"You're right," Rebecca said. Time to be optimistic, like Jenna. She rose to her feet. "Okay, I have another idea." She eased past him and into the bedroom, picking at her thumbnail. The next step might be a tough sell.

Nick followed. "Are you gonna tell me?"

"Okay." Rebecca faced him. "Clara also wrote about burying something under a willow by the creek."

"Burying what?"

"Well." She paused. Since he'd thought finding the rest of the diary was far-fetched, she had no clue how he'd react to this. "Some kind of box. And she said something about marking the spot with a symbol, and that it was under a willow tree."

"Seriously," Nick said flatly. "Like an X marks the spot. Like a treasure?"

"Well, it might say treasure box, but it might not. I couldn't read the exact words. The ink was smudged. Like it might have said *curse*, too, but maybe—" Rebecca clamped her mouth shut. She hadn't meant to tell him that part.

"Curse?" Nick said. "Come on."

"Never mind, the point is, maybe Clara hid the rest of the diary pages in the box, and that's what she wants me to find. Now that I think about it, the wind that I saw go through the corn could've stopped at the creek. I mean, I didn't actually see it go through the woods to this house, so . . ."

Nick stared at her for a painfully long moment. Rebecca's hopes withered. She'd lost him.

"Uh . . ." he said. "Okay. I really don't think there are gold doubloons around here."

"Right." She bowed her head. That was it. She was on her own.

"But it wouldn't hurt to look, I guess," Nick said. "Where's this creek?"

He was still in, at least for now. Rebecca suppressed a grin.

Together they trekked out of the house and through the backyard. As they entered the woods that led downhill to the creek, Rebecca's nerves tingled. The dense treetops blocked most of the daylight, leaving the world eerily murky. Something rustled through the underbrush behind them, and she got the uneasy feeling they were being followed. But no one knew they were at Meadow Winds, and there was no sign of old Mr. Schmidt. Then she spied a small black creature shadowing them.

Jade. Of course.

A curious rushing sound arose ahead. Rebecca picked up her pace and broke free from the trees. "Whoa," she said.

The creek wasn't a creek anymore. The trickling

ribbon of shallow water she'd waded through days before had swollen to three times its size, tumbling by at a crazy-fast speed.

"I never even knew this was back here," said Nick.

"All the rain must've flooded it." Rebecca peered right and left. There wasn't a willow tree in sight.

"I don't see any—"

"It could be farther down the bank," Rebecca said, trying to keep her hopes up. "Or there could be just a stump left."

"Rebecca, how are we supposed to know a willow stump from any other kind of stump?"

"I don't know," she admitted. "But please try. Keep your eye out for any Xs or symbols, too."

"Aye, aye, Captain," Nick said.

They parted ways, Rebecca going in one direction, Nick in the other, along the creek bank. Her heart sank lower with every step. There were trees but no willows. There were plenty of weeds, scrubby bushes, and wildflowers, but no stumps. And she didn't find anything that could be an X or a symbol.

After about five minutes, she wheeled around and saw Nick far off near a massive trunk that had fallen across the creek. He was coming her way.

"You know," he called, "if it was cut down fifty years ago or something, there probably wouldn't be any stump left."

"See any Xs?" Rebecca called back half-heartedly. "Or symbols?"

"Nope. Plenty of poison ivy, though. Watch out."

"What does it look like?" A gust of wind jostled the trees behind her.

"Three leaves clumped together on the same stalk."

Rebecca checked the ground by her feet. There were tons of weeds, but none with leaves like Nick described. Where she stood, the bank jutted out into the water, forcing the creek into a wide U-shaped bend. Below the bend the creek's surface was smooth, protected by the land from the water hurtling downstream. Her image reflected up at her—bare legs, shorts, and T-shirt, strands of dark hair escaping her ponytail holder and waving around her head in the wind.

As she watched her reflection, the water's rush faded to a murmur. The wind ceased. A buzz filled the air. Rebecca found herself hypnotized, unable to pull her eyes away from the creek. Suddenly her hair wasn't the only thing moving in the image before her. From the water's depths, a second shadow climbed to the surface, one that mirrored her own shape and size. She caught a flash of white. A face.

Rebecca floundered backward with a strangled scream, and the shadowy image in the water moved along with her, as if it were the reflection of someone who'd snuck up behind her. She spun around, but no one was there.

"Nick!" She whirled back to the creek. The face was still there. Long hair billowed around it like seaweed, hiding the eyes but not the mouth. The lips parted, opening wider and wider in a silent scream. "Nick!"

He hurried to her side. "What is it?"

"Do you see it? The face?" Rebecca's voice quavered as she pointed at the water.

"Where?"

"There, straight down. There's hair, and a mouth, it's right . . ."

Something dark blotted out the face, and Rebecca's reflection was alone. The water gushed louder than ever.

Nick placed his hand on her shoulder. "Rebecca. There's nothing there."

"But there was! It could've been Clara, I swear."

"I didn't see anything." His hand fell to his side.

"But . . . but how could you not see her?" Rebecca stammered. "She was so clear."

"I don't know what to tell you," Nick said.

"Well, there must be a reason you couldn't see her. I mean, you've seen evidence of the ghost before. Maybe

I can see her because I'm related to her." Rebecca nodded vigorously, trying to convince herself. "Or it could be part of the curse, like a warning to stay away."

"Maybe." Nick took a step backward. "Look. I gotta go to my game."

"Fine." Rebecca picked up a stick and began poking the muddy earth. If she was lucky, maybe she'd find the box.

Nick started up the hill. "You coming?"

"No. I want to look around a little more." She had no idea when she'd get another chance to look for the X. She jabbed the ground harder. The stick broke.

Nick paused. "You should leave, too. Come watch my game."

"No, thanks," Rebecca said, flinging the useless stick to the ground. "I don't want to watch anything. I want to do something."

"Well, don't stay too long," Nick said. "You don't want to get caught again. I'll text you when I can, okay?"

"Sure. Whatever." She turned her back to him and watched the creek flow. After a moment, Nick's footsteps shuffled away.

Rebecca found a fallen log to sit on, but before she did, she rolled it over to make sure there was no X underneath. There wasn't. She plopped down dejectedly. The pieces of the puzzle she'd hoped to find—the rest of the diary and whatever Clara had buried under the willow—were still hidden, maybe gone forever. She was getting nowhere.

She wished with all she had that she could talk to Mom. Part of her wanted to share everything that had been going on with the ghost and Clara's diary. But part of her feared Mom wouldn't listen. And another part wanted to hide it all, to punish Mom for not believing. It would serve her right.

Rebecca sat awhile, lost in thought, until a twig snapped. She craned around to see Jade inching noiselessly toward her, laser-focused on something behind the fallen log. Rebecca's skin crawled. Cats could sense ghosts, according to *Heart-Stopping Heartland Hauntings*. Rebecca imagined the thing in the creek emerging, dripping, reaching for her. She whirled around.

A face moved between the branches of a bush.

Rebecca gasped and scrabbled to a crouch. The bush shook. Someone giggled.

Kelsie.

Red-hot anger scorched through Rebecca. She lurched to her feet. "What are you doing?"

Kelsie emerged, her skinny frame convulsing with laughter. "Oh my God, that was too funny. You are such a wimp."

"And you're such a loser," Rebecca said, clenching her fists. "Spying on me! Why are you here?"

"None of your business." Kelsie smirked. "Oh, and I'm a loser? You're the one trespassing. Again."

"I don't think your grandpa wants you here, either," Rebecca shot back.

"Whatever. I won't tell if you don't."

They stared each other down. Kelsie looked worse than ever, her eyes bloodshot and her usually smooth hair unbrushed. Jade, hovering near Rebecca's feet, hissed, her one eye a slit. Kelsie's tough act dropped. She stepped back.

"Sorry, I can't control her," Rebecca said.

"You need to leave," Kelsie said. "And take the cat with you."

"Look." Rebecca tried a new tactic. "My family used to own this property and built that house."

"So?"

"Well, wouldn't you be curious about this place if you were me?"

"Nope. Ancient history. Which is boring, like I told you before."

A wave of exhaustion swamped Rebecca. She didn't want to fight with Kelsie anymore. "Fine. You know what? It's okay that we're not friends. But we should try to get along if we're going to see each other around this summer."

"Why?" Kelsie's jaw tightened.

"Well, our parents—"

"*My* parents are getting back together!"

Jade yowled and sprang at Kelsie, who gave a strangled cry and took off.

"Why is that cat always after me?" she yelled over her shoulder. "Get out of here and take her with you!" She fled into the trees.

Jade purred at Rebecca, then calmly set off toward Meadow Winds. Rebecca fell in step behind her. Once again, the cat seemed to be on her side. According to *Heart-Stopping Heartland Hauntings*, cats could sniff out evil.

Kelsie might not be evil, but Jade sure didn't like her.

SIXTEEN

No one said much at dinner. The rain had started again, which made everyone cranky. Justin whined and wouldn't eat. Aunt Sylvie kept shifting in her chair, one hand on her swollen belly. Even in the air-conditioning, the humidity made wisps of Rebecca's hair escape her ponytail, tickling her cheeks and clinging to her neck.

"Hey, guys," Aunt Sylvie said as the meal ended. "If the weather clears up, why don't we hit the county fair tomorrow. It'd be fun. We can get some cotton candy, ride a few rides, listen to live music."

Thunder boomed outside.

"Seems like a big *if*," Mom said.

"Cand-dee, can-dee," chanted Justin.

"I checked the forecast," Uncle Jon said. "Supposed to be overcast, but no rain. It'll be muddy, though."

Aunt Sylvie sighed. "The news said this has been the rainiest July around here in over a hundred years."

"I wouldn't doubt it," said Mom. Lightning flashed through the window behind her.

Rebecca pushed her coleslaw around her plate. In her diary Clara had written about a rainy July and how awful it had been. In "Signs of the Ghost," Dad had written that the ghost showed up when it was raining or about to rain. She wondered if there was a connection.

"The farmers are worried," Uncle Jon said. "Crops had been growing like crazy until the last few weeks. But now the fields are all swampy and the rivers rising. Hopefully there won't be any flash floods."

"It's tornado season now, too," said Mom.

A tiny knot of dread formed in Rebecca's chest. All the rain wasn't just dreary; it could also be dangerous. She hadn't really thought of it that way until now.

Before bed, she picked up *Heart-Stopping Heartland Hauntings,* which had gotten to be a habit. It reassured her to know that she wasn't the only person who'd ever experienced a ghost. Rebecca wasn't sure if it was smart to use the book as a resource, but every time she read a chapter she found out some new information. Sometimes it helped her, but sometimes it just added to her confusion.

Usually it scared her.

Tonight's tale was called simply "The Punisher." The title alone gave Rebecca a stab of fear. The first line read:

It is not wise to disturb a ghost.

It was about a group of paranormal investigators in the 1970s who camped out in an abandoned Ohio penitentiary for a week, trying to capture proof it was haunted. Rumor had it the ghost of a man hanged for murder wandered its halls. The team took photos using bright flashes, set up a lot of equipment, constantly yelled questions, and ended up provoking the ghost so much that it snapped. It transformed from an eerie but harmless shadow into a violent force that smashed their equipment and chased the terrified team into the nearby half-frozen river, almost killing them.

Yikes. The story kept Rebecca awake for hours. It was one of those rare nights since she'd been in Iowa that no rain pattered on the windows. She'd gotten so used to the sound, she couldn't seem to fall asleep without it. The silence was deafening. When a typical nighttime noise did pop up—a faraway train horn or a cricket chirping—it seemed way too loud.

Worse were the noises Rebecca didn't want to hear. A scritch-scratch in the walls. The eerie hoot of an owl. The faint creaking of the ropes holding the swing under the maple. She thought about covering her head with her pillow, but then if something snuck into her room she wouldn't know until it was too late.

Around 1:00 a.m. two sharp raps struck the front window. Rebecca's heart skipped. She lifted her head. The raps hit again, once, twice. There weren't any tree branches close enough to the house to touch the glass. Could it be a bird? She hesitated, then slipped out of bed and tiptoed to the window. Gathering her courage, she parted the curtains.

Nothing was there except for a full moon high in the sky, casting a ghostly glow over the countryside. Then a sudden gust of wind shook the pane, making the crystal sun catcher hit the glass. Rebecca's fear melted away. So that's what the sound had been. A beam of moonlight passed through the sun catcher, highlighting some marks on the surface. Curious, she lifted it from its hook and switched on her bedside lamp.

Etched into the middle facet were two tiny hearts, side by side.

A low rumble erupted in the hall. Rebecca peered past her open door. A black shape, low to the ground, slithered toward her.

It was Jade. Purring.

Rebecca switched off her light. That cat sure was

sneaky. As Rebecca hung the sun catcher back in place, Jade began weaving in and around her ankles. Rebecca leaned down to pet her soft fur, but the cat twisted out of reach and padded away. She stopped at the door and looked back at Rebecca, tail twitching.

Rebecca's skin tingled. Jade was acting exactly like she had the day she'd led her to Meadow Winds. "Be brave," she whispered to herself.

She followed the cat down the steps to the first floor, into the kitchen, and straight to the back door. Jade meowed and scratched the wood. Rebecca let her out. The night air was thick and hot. Heat lightning flickered in distant clouds. The yard was strange and lonely in the pale light of the moon. Her family upstairs seemed very far away.

Jade trotted straight to the barn.

"Okay, let's do this," Rebecca said matter-of-factly, hoping the sound of her voice would give her courage. It didn't.

The grass scratched her bare feet as she sneaked across the yard. The barn's side door was a yawning black rectangle in the wall. She shot an uneasy glance at the swing, which wobbled ever so slightly under the maple. The cornfields silently watched her progress.

When she finally reached the barn, Rebecca took a

tentative step inside. Jade crouched near a bin, her one eye glittering in the moonlight, then melted away into the darkness.

Rebecca steeled herself and ventured deeper inside, until blackness engulfed her. She could barely see. A shadow loomed to her left and she gasped—a figure lurked under the hayloft. She half turned, ready to flee, then realized it was just a ladder. She dug her fingernails into her palms. A tiny meow came from the direction of Mom's office. She crept toward the sound.

Suddenly the crushing chill of the ghost overwhelmed her, taking her breath and freezing her muscles until she couldn't budge. Next to the office doorway, a white blur almost like a fog gathered near the floor. As Rebecca watched, terrified, the fog twisted and rose, morphing into a vertical column. It pulsed and took shape—an arm here, a shoulder there, a head on top, each protruding one at a time then sinking back into the fog.

"What do you want?" Rebecca choked out the words.

The shape wavered, and the garbled whispering started.

"I can't understand you," Rebecca said desperately. Something thudded in Mom's office and a small black object scuttled across the threshold floor right toward her. She stumbled backward, crashed into a bin, and fell to the concrete. The ghost surged forward, now the shape of a whole person, one hand clutching its throat, the other thrusting at Rebecca's neck.

She screamed. There was a burst of lightning outside, and the air crackled with electricity. Thunder roared, obliterating the whispers. The ghost vanished.

Rebecca clambered to her feet and tore out of the barn. The wind whipped, and the swing danced crazily under the maple. She got back in the house as fast as she could and locked the door behind her.

The rest of the night Rebecca huddled in bed petrified, waiting for another heavy rush of air to swamp her and the ghost to appear. Every time she drifted off, she jerked awake, terrified the dream would come.

She had to face facts. The ghost wasn't the same sad shadow from back in Dad's day. His signs of the ghost were minor compared to what was happening to her. Now the ghost could whisper, slam doors, push heavy trunks. And appear in a humanlike form. Its frustration was growing. What if it snapped, like the "Punisher" ghost in the Ohio penitentiary? Maybe it would hurt her. It had come straight at her holding its neck. Did it want to strangle her? A line from *Heart-Stopping Heartland Hauntings* kept running through her thoughts.

Beware the ghost that changes its behavior for the worse.
Often this is a sign of growing disturbance and malice.

Rebecca curled into a ball. She had no idea what the ghost would do next.

And danger seemed to be rushing closer and closer.

SEVENTEEN

The sun shone the next day for the first time in forever. As soon as the minivan door slid open in the fairgrounds parking lot, Rebecca started searching the crowd for Nick. They'd texted the night before and he'd said he'd probably be at the fair, too, but he hadn't answered her text that morning. Of course she'd mentioned seeing the ghost, but she could hardly wait to tell him the whole story in person.

He wouldn't be easy to find, though. Everyone in the county must've decided to make the most of the dry weather. Hordes of people streamed toward the ticket gates—from gray-haired ladies with walkers to bald-headed babies in strollers to hulking high school jocks jostling and pushing through the crowd. Carnival music and distorted loudspeaker announcements added to the chaos. Hanging over everything—the stinky combo of fried dough, cow manure, and underarm sweat.

"Pee-yoo!" said Justin, plugging his nose with his fingertips as the group entered the fairgrounds.

Aunt Sylvie turned green. "I'll take Justin over to the kiddie rides," she said. "Maybe I can catch some fresh air there."

"Good luck, honey." Uncle Jon grinned and passed out flyers with a map and schedule of events. "I want to check out the rhubarb pie contest. Christine, Becks, wanna come along?"

"Sure," Mom said.

"Actually, I want to check out the horses. Can I meet you guys later?"

"Tell you what," said Uncle Jon. He pointed at bleachers rising to the sky on the other side of the fairgrounds. "There's a good local band playing at the grandstand in an hour. Let's meet at the entrance."

The group split up, and Rebecca meandered along the midway toward the barns, relieved to be on her own. She kept her eyes peeled for Nick, but there was no sign of him.

The horses took her mind off her problems for a bit. She liked comparing the beautiful animals and reading their quirky names written on the stall doors. She'd only ridden a horse once. Jenna was probably riding every single day and getting really good at it. Jealousy stabbed her. She pushed the feeling away.

After twenty minutes, Rebecca exited the barn onto an avenue of booths displaying all sorts of art. She wandered along, absentmindedly checking out the pottery and paintings while scanning the crowd for Nick. Finally, past a long line of fair-goers waiting in front of a big white tent, she spotted a familiar Dodgers baseball cap. Nick was walking toward her, munching on a huge swirl of pink cotton candy. He hadn't seen her yet. As Rebecca opened her mouth to call his name, Kelsie popped out from the line of people between them and waved enthusiastically at Nick.

"Hey!" Kelsie yelled. "Come keep me company. I've been standing here forever!"

Rebecca immediately dodged into the booth next to her and hid behind a large easel. If she'd been four steps ahead, she would've run smack into Kelsie. She held her breath and listened.

"Hi, Kelsie." Nick's raspy voice carried over the chatter of the other fair-goers. "What are you doing?"

"They're appraising antiques here and maybe buying them," Kelsie said. "I'm trying to find out how much cash I can get for this."

Rebecca didn't want to get caught eavesdropping, but she peeked around the easel. Directly in front of her stood a red-haired woman holding a mantel clock, and beyond her was Kelsie, holding out what looked like a heart-shaped gold locket for Nick's inspection. Rebecca ducked back behind the easel and pretended to study its display of scenic photos.

"Where'd you get that?" Nick asked.

"It's a family heirloom," Kelsie said. "It's solid gold, so I'm sure it's worth a ton."

"What's S.C.?"

"Oh. Yeah. Those were my grandmother's initials," Kelsie said. "On my mom's side. Susannah Cooper. See, there are some pictures of her inside. Wasn't she adorable?"

"I guess," Nick said. Rebecca snickered. She'd never met a boy her age who wanted to talk about babies. "Why do you want to sell it? I mean, won't your family get mad?"

"No, it's mine now. I have it, so I can do what I want with it."

Rebecca pursed her lips. Typical Kelsie.

An ear-piercing ringtone sounded. Rebecca glanced at the mostly middle-aged couples discussing which piece of artwork in the booth would fit best over their couches. No one grabbed their phone.

"Oh, no, I gotta meet my dad in five minutes," Kelsie

said. Rebecca snorted. Of course the obnoxious ringtone belonged to Kelsie. "Great. Now I'll have to wait until we come back tomorrow night to get rid of this thing."

The ringtone rang out again.

"Yuck, are you kidding me?" Kelsie whined. "We're meeting at the grandstand to hear a band. With Rebecca and her family."

"What's so bad about that?" Nick asked.

"Oh, she is so jealous of me," Kelsie said. "It's totally obvious."

"What?" Rebecca hissed. A lady next to her in a straw hat gave her the side-eye.

"Really?" Nick said.

"Oh, totally. Plus, she's immature," Kelsie said. "I mean, she talks about ghosts all the time. It's weird right?"

"A little," Nick said.

Rebecca stiffened.

"Why are you friends with her, anyway?" Kelsie asked. "Do you feel sorry for her, 'cause her dad died?"

"Well, yeah, of course," Nick said. "I mean it'd be awful not to have a dad."

Rebecca flinched, like she'd been kicked in the gut. Was that why Nick was her friend—because he felt bad for her? His pity was worse than Kelsie's nastiness. She felt sick.

"Whatever," Kelsie said. "I gotta go. You wanna walk with me?"

Rebecca braced herself, ready to run to the back of the booth if they came her way.

"It's almost time for me to leave, actually," Nick said.

"Oh, okay. Tell you what." Kelsie's tone turned border-line flirty. "Why don't you come explore Meadow Winds with me tomorrow?"

"Where?"

"Don't give me that. I know you've been there with Rebecca before. She told me. I've found a bunch of arrow-heads from the Sioux tribe around there. It's a cool place to hang out when you're bored."

"Maybe." Nick's voice wavered.

"Three o'clock tomorrow? My dad and grandpa will be here at the fair." Kelsie kept pushing. "I want to check out the barn. Maybe find something interesting before it gets torn down."

"I have a baseball game at twelve. If it's over by then—"

"Well, I'll be there no matter what. Later!"

Rebecca plunged toward the back of the booth to hide, in case they looked her way. In her hurry she crashed into another easel. A man in a straw hat with a fair badge pinned to his chest sprang at her.

"Watch out, young lady," he said, steadying the easel.

"Sorry, sorry," she said, trying to help him.

"Rebecca?" It was Nick, behind her.

Busted. Rebecca turned. Nick stood with a stunned expression at the entrance to the booth.

"Sorry," she mumbled again to the man. She marched over to Nick and blurted the first thing that came to mind. "We don't need to be friends just because you feel sorry for me."

Nick paled. "You heard that?"

"Yes." Rebecca wrapped her arms around herself.

"I don't feel sorry for you." Nick crumpled his empty cotton candy stick in his fist. "I mean, I do feel bad about your dad, but that's not why I'm your friend."

"Are you sure?" The pulsing bass line from the music of a nearby carnival ride pounded in her head. A young mom carrying a crying toddler stepped awkwardly around them.

"Come over here." Nick pulled Rebecca away from the crowd and behind the row of booths. A scrawny tree offered a small spot of shade. "I do like hanging out with you. I didn't know what to say to her. I'm sorry." He looked genuinely miserable.

Rebecca wasn't ready to forgive him yet. "If you were really my friend, you would stick up for me."

"You're right. I wimped out." He shoved his hands into his pockets. "How can I make it up to you?"

Rebecca chewed her lip. Kelsie did have a way of barreling over other people. And she didn't want to be in a fight with Nick. She wanted and needed his help. She puffed out a breath. "Okay. Fine. Did you get my text? About the ghost in the barn?"

"Oh. Yeah."

"So." Rebecca geared up to share her idea. "I have a new theory."

"Really?" Nick said dubiously. "I don't know—"

"Just listen a minute." She grabbed his hands. "Maybe if we take a shovel back to where I saw the face in the creek and dig there, we'll find the treasure."

"Rebecca." Nick wore a slight smile, enough for the dimple in his cheek to appear. Her heart lurched. She'd forced herself to forget how cute he was so she wouldn't get nervous around him, but the evidence was staring right at her.

He gently wiggled his hands out of hers. Heat blasted into her cheeks. Oh, no. What if he thought she'd been holding hands because she had a crush on him? She shoved her fists into her pockets.

"Look," Nick said, "I know you think Clara says she made an X to mark the spot, but we can't find it. Even if it was ever there, it's not there anymore." His smile faded. "And you aren't serious about digging up the whole creek bank, right?"

"Well . . ." Uh-oh. This wasn't going to be good.

Nick rubbed the toe of his basketball shoe in some sawdust. "I don't want to be a jerk or anything, but you know this is all kind of crazy, right?"

"Oh." All the air seeped from Rebecca's lungs with that one sound. "I thought you wanted to help me."

"I do." Nick's eyes stayed fixed on the ground. "It's been really fun—"

"Fun?" He was acting like she was a little kid playing games, and he'd only been humoring her. She took a step back. "Oh, I get it. Right. You were only hanging out with me to prove I was wrong. To find a scientific explanation."

"No, that's not true. It's just, forget whether or not ghosts exist—"

"They do."

"Okay, but why would a ghost want you to find a box? You don't really think it's full of treasure, do you? And if you believe you're supposed to find it, do you really believe Clara put a curse on it? 'Cause then why would you want to find it and get cursed?" He threw up his hands. "None of this makes sense."

"Yes, but I might've been wrong." Rebecca had to

convince him. "I've been thinking—what if Clara's mom is the ghost? Eleanor! Maybe she started haunting Clara that summer of 1900 and that's what she was so upset about in the diary? The face in the creek could totally have been Eleanor's. Clara didn't really look like her dad, so she probably looked like her mom. If Eleanor is the ghost—"

"But why would she haunt her own daughter?" Nick shook his head. "That'd be . . . mean."

"Okay, maybe not haunting, maybe watching over her." Rebecca spoke quickly. "Clara wrote about how sad she was, and how her father never wanted to talk. And about how she'd go to the willow tree and hear the wind whisper or something and know she wasn't alone. Maybe Eleanor appeared that summer to Clara!"

Nick folded his arms. "But that doesn't explain why the ghost would be around now."

"Something must've disturbed it." Rebecca began to pace in a circle. "It's way stronger than when my dad saw it, it's moving stuff and, like, visible now."

"Rebecca," Nick said. "It seems like you're kinda making it up as you go along."

She scudded to a stop. "I'm not making this up!"

"I know you believe all this." Nick raked a hand through his hair. "But, I think, maybe, you're seeing things because you want to. I don't know, 'cause of your dad or something?"

"Seeing the ghost has nothing to do with my dad! It was really there!"

"Okay, okay, but maybe you should talk to your mom about this stuff."

Rebecca's heart hardened. "You think I have problems."

"No, that's not it."

"But you feel sorry for me. That's what you told Kelsie."

"No! Please don't get mad. Just think about it—"

"Fine." Everything he'd said to Kelsie had been true. Rebecca turned her back so he wouldn't see her falling apart. "I don't need you. Forget it." She stalked away, holding her head high.

"Rebecca!" Nick called.

She kept going and lost herself in the crowd.

A few minutes later, Rebecca found herself in front of a brightly painted carousel. The spinning horses were only splotches of color through the tears stinging her eyes.

She'd never be able to convince Nick there was a ghost. That goal had been doomed from the start.

He had never really been on her side.

EiGHTEEN

The rest of the family had fun at the concert, but Rebecca, sitting as far away from Kelsie as possible, hardly heard a note played. She was too upset at Nick's betrayal to enjoy herself. When the rain held off again the next day and everyone wanted to go back to the fair, she pretended she had a headache. She wanted to be alone.

After her family left, Rebecca collapsed miserably on the purple couch in the living room. Uncle Jon and Aunt Sylvie were great and everything, but they had too much going on in their own lives to really care about her. Jenna might as well be on the moon she was so far away and out of touch. Nick, the one friend she thought she'd made in Iowa, had given up on her. Kelsie hated her guts. Mom ignored her for Mark. Dad was gone.

Rebecca had no one.

Her nightmare from the night before kept repeating in her mind. This time she'd tripped over tombstones while running through the storm, willow branches thrashing at her. A hand had clamped onto her shoulder, and not the soothing hand that helped wake her out of dreams. When she'd turned to confront whoever it was, strands of pale hair rushed at her, twisting like snakes. Lightning flashed, showing Clara—or maybe Eleanor—eyes vacant and staring, one hand still digging into Rebecca, the other clawing at her own throat.

Rebecca pressed her fingers to her eyes, trying to erase the images. The ghost, whoever it was, had invaded her dreams. But she still couldn't figure out what it wanted from her. She was only twelve years old. There was no way she could stop the demolition of Meadow Winds, if that was what it was so mad about. She'd tried to find the diary and whatever had been buried by the creek but hadn't been able to. She'd vowed to solve the mystery of the ghost, like her dad had wanted, but she was failing that mission.

Failing *him*.

"Sorry, Dad," Rebecca whispered. "I can't do it."

She felt the weight of his disappointment, or maybe her own, pushing down on her. If she couldn't stop the ghost, what would it do next with its growing strength? It'd better not go after Justin.

The thought shocked Rebecca like a lightning strike. She couldn't let anything happen to her little cousin, or anyone else in the Graff family. They had just started to get to know each other. She forced herself to a seated position. No way could she quit yet. She owed it to Dad and to her family to give all the clues at least one more look.

The envelope from Clara's trunk lay on the coffee table in front of her. Rebecca opened it and poured out the contents, the diary pages and photos landing in a heap. She wasn't sure where to begin. She'd studied everything a kazillion times and hadn't learned anything new. Picking up the last diary page, the one with the blurred ink, she ran her fingers over the distorted, bumpy words. It was as if water had spilled on the paper. Or tears.

She closed her eyes. Of course it had been tears. Clara's sadness had literally marked the pages. She had to be missing something. If only Clara had left a treasure map.

Rebecca's eyes flew open. Maybe there was a treasure map. Mom always said a picture was worth a thousand words. She grabbed the torn photo, the one she'd found under the window seat at Meadow Winds. "Yes!"

How could she not have seen it before? What she'd thought were vines hanging next to Clara's blurry face were actually willow branches. If she took the photo to the creek, maybe she could figure out where it had been taken, judging by the angle of the roof and chimney in the picture. Then she'd know where the willow had stood and could dig for whatever it was that was buried there.

Rebecca crammed the photo into her back pocket and raced out of the house.

Minutes later, she'd cut through the cornfields and was at the creek. The fallen tree made a perfect bridge. She picked her way across, holding her arms wide to keep her balance, concentrating on counting her steps instead of looking into the swirling, mud-brown water. The thought of falling in made her knees wobble. It took seven steps to get to the other side.

Rebecca jumped to the ground and dug the photo out of her pocket. Holding it up, she squinted over its top edge, comparing the image in the photo to the reality in front of her. The trees had changed a ton in a hundred years and, from where she was, almost completely blocked the house. Her plan might not work. She veered upstream and kept trying.

After about ten minutes Rebecca was sweating and

discouraged. She'd even tried the exact spot where she'd seen the face in the creek, but the roof looked totally different from there compared to the photo. Finally, she neared a large patch of poison ivy. Getting as close as she could without touching the leaves, she held up the photo and gazed toward Meadow Winds. Her heart soared.

She'd found the spot.

In her excitement, her feet slipped in the mud and she lost her balance. She threw her weight toward the creek, trying to miss the poison ivy, and bashed into a prickly bush. Her hip struck a hard object. She twisted to see what it was, and her heart faltered.

In the middle of the overgrown bush lurked a gravestone.

Rebecca lurched to her feet, energy surging through her. She stomped at the brambles, smashing them down until she'd cleared a space around the stone, then bent low to get a better view.

Only a small portion wasn't covered by moss.

Died July 28, 1900

God gives us angels and He takes them away.

An alarm bell went off in Rebecca's brain: *1900?* That was the year of Clara's journal. She seized a stick and scraped at the stone. Flecks of moss and dirt crumbled away. More letters and numbers emerged.

ara ine Foxx

Born May 14, 1888

Rebecca's fingers quivered. Wasn't that Clara's birthday? But she hadn't died until she was an old lady. Cold sweat stung her forehead. She continued to chip away with the stick.

Evange

She rubbed furiously and the final letter appeared, the one at the beginning of the name.

S

Sara

Sara Evangeline Foxx

Clara had a twin sister.

Dazed, Rebecca fell back on her heels. Bursts of wind swirled around her, but she hardly noticed. The puzzle pieces snapped into place—the photo torn in half, the heartbreaking diary, why this spot under the willow had been important to Clara.

Sara had died in 1900. When she and Clara were twelve years old. That was the tragedy that blew up Clara's life and made her so sad. Losing her sister.

Her *twin.*

The ghost wasn't Clara or Eleanor or a Schmidt. It was Sara.

The rush of the creek filled Rebecca's ears. Her eyes fell on a flat, thin rock about the size of a platter half-wedged under the bush. One side of it was partially sunk in mud, the other stuck up slightly into the air. The surface of the rock was etched, like someone had drawn on it. She scooted closer.

Two hearts were carved in its middle, exactly like those on the sun catcher in her room. The inside of one read "C & S" and the inside of the other read "S & C."

Rebecca tensed. Did those letters stand for Clara and Sara?

Sara and Clara?

S.C.?

She gasped. Those letters, in that order, rang a bell. She'd just heard them. Nick had asked Kelsie what the S.C. on her locket—her *heart-shaped* locket—stood for. A horrible suspicion crawled across her brain. Sure, lots of people had those initials, but it'd be a pretty big coincidence if Kelsie's grandma's initials were the same as those on this rock.

Images clicked through her mind: Kelsie's dirty fingernails, the necklace disappearing under her shirt, the mud-caked shoes in her bedroom.

Maybe the hearts and initials on the rock marked the

spot where Clara's treasure box had been buried. "Under the willow where it belongs," like the diary had said. Next to Sara's grave.

A treasure for a twelve-year-old girl probably wouldn't be gold doubloons, as Nick had pointed out. But it absolutely could be a gold locket with the initials belonging to her and her twin.

Rebecca leapt to her feet. What if Kelsie had dug up the box and taken the treasure for herself? That could be what had disturbed Sara's ghost, what was making it angry. It must be close to three o'clock. Kelsie could be on her way to meet Nick at Meadow Winds. In a few hours she would take the locket to the antique appraisal at the fair and try to sell it.

Rebecca had to get that locket. Now.

NINETEEN

As Rebecca raced into the backyard at Meadow Winds, an eye-searing burst of lightning and massive boom of thunder jolted her to the core. She searched the sky. The flat gray clouds had gone, replaced by towering black thunderheads. In an instant, the clouds opened and rain drenched her hair, her face, her clothes.

Staggering toward the house, she collided with someone. Nick.

"Come on!" He yelled, latching on to her wrist.

Rebecca didn't think twice. Together they dashed across the yard, their feet kicking up mud behind them. Within seconds they launched themselves through the back door and into the kitchen.

Rebecca skidded to a stop and fell against a wall,

gulping in air. Nick ripped off his sopping wet baseball cap and shook his head like a puppy. Water droplets flew.

"I've never seen a storm come up that fast before," she said, panting.

Nick leaned over, his hands on his knees. He swiped his forearm across his dripping face. "Me neither."

The house swayed and moaned in the wind. Shadows obscured every corner.

Nick jammed his cap back on his head. "Rebecca. I—"

A ripping crash reverberated above, and a chunk of plaster dropped from the ceiling. Sticky air swooshed at them from the front of the house.

"The roof!" Rebecca pushed away from the wall. "Come on!"

She seized Nick's hand and dragged him outside. A blast of wind almost knocked her over, but she lowered her head and plowed around the corner of the house. Reaching the cellar doors, she yanked one of the handles, but her hand slid off the slippery metal. Nick got a grip and tugged, and for one awful second the door wouldn't budge. Then suddenly it flew open, and they tumbled inside seconds before it slammed shut, barely missing their skulls.

The cellar was pitch-black, the air stifling and hushed. Rebecca slumped on the steps next to Nick, panting. "Okay, I think we're safe in here."

A slight rustle made her freeze.

"What's that?" Nick whispered.

"Shhhh." Rebecca grabbed his knee, warning him to be still, and strained her ears, trying to ignore the muffled sounds of the storm. If they were trapped in the cellar with a terrified raccoon or something, they could be in as much trouble now as they had been in the house.

The rustle came again. The thin line of light coming from between the cellar doors barely lit the room, but Rebecca's eyes were adjusting to the darkness.

A figure stood in the corner.

Rebecca shrieked. Nick jerked to his feet.

Someone giggled. "God, it's so easy to scare you."

A mix of relief and rage flooded Rebecca. "Kelsie."

"Duh," Kelsie said, moving forward, her yellow rain jacket glowing faintly. "What did you think, that I was a ghost? What a joke."

There was a click, then a light pierced Rebecca's eyes. She threw her hands up to block the glare. "Stop it!"

"Oh, my bad," Kelsie said sweetly, and pointed the flashlight at the floor. "Nick, what's she doing here? I didn't invite her."

"Don't be like that, Kelsie," Nick said.

"Why not? This is *my* family's property, not hers. Nothing here belongs to them." Her hand scrabbled to the chain around her neck, almost like she wanted to make sure it was still there.

Like she wanted to protect it from being taken away.

Like it didn't really belong to her.

In that moment Rebecca knew for sure. And she was done with Kelsie's games. "Where'd you really get that necklace?" she demanded.

Next to her, Nick stirred in surprise, but Rebecca stopped him with a nudge to the ribs.

"I told you," Kelsie said, jerking her hand away from the chain as if it burned. "It's from my mom."

"I don't believe you," Rebecca said, fighting to stay calm.

Kelsie flipped a lock of her hair over her shoulder. "That's your problem."

Rebecca rocketed to her feet and down the steps. "I think you found it under a rock at the creek. I think it belonged to one of my ancestors, Sara Foxx. You dug up a box from where it was buried next to her grave and you took it for yourself."

"Um, Rebecca?" Nick said. "What are you talking about?"

Kelsie laughed and backed up. "She has no clue." Her voice shook slightly.

"Really?" Rebecca said. "So if I asked your dad about

that locket, he'd tell me you got it from your mom?" Even in the dim light, she saw Kelsie's whole body go rigid.

"You keep away from my dad," she said through clenched teeth.

"Whoa, okay, calm down," Nick said.

"No!" Kelsie yelled. "You know what? My dad and I were fine until Rebecca and her mom came along. In fact, he and *my* mom were about to get back together, I could just tell, but her mom ruined it! Ever since they showed up, everything's been going wrong, I can't sleep, I have nightmares—"

"How is that our fault?" Rebecca said. The cellar doors rattled in the wind above.

"Listen." Nick jumped down the steps and spread his arms between them, keeping them apart. "Kelsie, what's going on?"

Kelsie pressed her lips together, her eyes darting from side to side. "It doesn't matter who used to own this locket. Meadow Winds and everything on it belongs to us now."

"So you did find it by the creek!" Rebecca said.

"Is that true, Kelsie?" Nick lowered his arms.

Kelsie planted her hands on her hips. "Fine. I'll tell, but only because *you* asked, Nick. I found a treasure box buried by the creek. The locket was in it."

"I knew it!" Rebecca shouted.

"But how did you find it?" Nick said. "We looked and looked."

"It was easy." Kelsie sneered. "I saw something metal sticking out of the bank, and I pulled it out. I didn't need an X to mark the spot."

"Hold on," Rebecca said. "Why are you calling it a treasure box and talking about Xs? How do you know—"

"I heard you!" Kelsie snorted. "I heard everything, all that junk about diaries and ghosts. I told you, this place is *my* spot, not yours!" The cellar doors again shook violently.

"You mean you've been spying on us?" Anger burned in Rebecca's chest. She remembered the clatter from the back bedroom the day she and Nick had found the torn photo. "So you were in the house, listening to us? *You* knocked over those boards that one day?"

"Yes! You thought it was a mouse?" Kelsie snickered. "I was hiding in the closet the whole time, but you were too dumb to look." She put her hand on Nick's arm. "I don't mean you, Nick. I get that you were playing along because you feel bad for Rebecca."

He pulled out of her grasp. "Kelsie, cut it out. Rebecca is my friend."

"Just give me the locket, Kelsie." Rebecca was over this.

"Nope. Finders keepers."

"But you stole it!"

"How could I steal it if it's on my grandpa's property?"

Rebecca balled up her fists. "Well, now you know the farm used to belong to my family, and that the locket belonged to one of my relatives. So hand it over."

"I don't know that. You're probably making it all up. You love to make up stuff. All that junk about ghosts. There is no such thing as a ghost!"

A deafening blast of thunder shook the ground. Rebecca's skin tingled, and a wave of dizziness passed through her. She swayed. Nick grabbed her elbow. The temperature in the cellar plunged.

Kelsie's sass evaporated. "What's wrong?" she asked wildly. "What's happening?"

The air thickened and pressed. A low buzz of energy hummed. White light blazed in the center of the cellar, and fog swirled into a shape.

Sara.

Kelsie shrieked and flattened herself against the dirt wall. Nick's fingers dug into Rebecca's arm. This time Rebecca wasn't scared, only curious.

The ghost was more substantial than before, her features more defined. Her face wore an expression of longing, which twisted into anger as her eyes fixed on Kelsie. She raised her arms—one hand to her throat and the other reaching out, exactly like she had in the barn.

Sara wanted her locket.

Kelsie squeezed her eyes closed. "There's no such thing, there's no such thing."

"Give me the locket, Kelsie," Rebecca said. "That's all she wants."

"No, no, no." Kelsie shook her head violently. "I found it for a reason. It was meant to be."

"What are you talking about?" Rebecca asked.

"I'm going to sell it and use the money to buy a bus ticket to go see my mom." Kelsie's voice rose higher and higher. "I can talk her into getting back with my dad. And nothing will stop me. Nothing!"

A flicker of compassion sparked deep inside Rebecca. In that moment, all her anger and frustration toward Kelsie crumbled. Kelsie missed her mom. And she wanted her parents together. Rebecca understood how that felt.

The whispering began, a frantic babble that made no sense. Sara's mouth gaped and her form grew larger and more solid, shimmering in the dank air. Kelsie whimpered and covered her ears.

"Please give me the locket," Rebecca begged. "I won't let her hurt you."

"No!" Kelsie yelled.

Without warning, Sara lunged at Kelsie, both arms reaching. Kelsie screamed and dashed the locket to the floor. As Rebecca scrambled to pick it up, Kelsie pushed past Nick and bolted up the stairs.

"Don't go out there!" he shouted.

Kelsie rammed her hands against the doors, and they flew open with a terrible groan. Wind whipped into the cellar and Kelsie teetered, almost falling backward, until she lowered her head, barreled forward, and fled into the storm.

With a hair-raising scream, Sara swooshed up the steps and vanished.

"Sara, no! I have the locket!" yelled Rebecca. From the open door came a crash of thunder.

Kelsie screamed, "Get away from me!"

Rebecca hurtled toward the stairs.

Nick snagged her arm, stopping her. "You can't go out there."

Rebecca hesitated. He was right. The locket was safe; she didn't need to risk her life. But she couldn't help feeling that this mess was partly her own fault. Maybe if she'd tried harder to befriend Kelsie, or been smart enough to understand what the ghost wanted, none of this would be happening. She wrenched free from Nick's grasp and tore up the steps, out of the cellar, and into the storm.

The wind howled and whirled around her, forcing her to stumble in circles. Trees bent sideways, leaves and branches hurtled by, rain pummeled her. She couldn't see Kelsie. She had to find her. Where was Sara? A sickening dread knotted Rebecca's stomach.

Then it hit her. She was trapped in her nightmare. And this time she couldn't wake up, because it was real.

Lightning slashed across the sky and illuminated the yellow raincoat bobbing underneath the huge oak in the front yard.

"Kelsie," Rebecca yelled. "Come back!"

Kelsie wheeled around, and her gaze flew past Rebecca. Her face contorted with terror. "No!"

Rebecca's hair crackled and stood on end. A cold hand clamped onto her shoulder, and a girl's anguished voice filled her head.

"Not again!"

For an instant, the world turned white and quiet. Then, as if in slow motion, Rebecca's senses cleared. A jagged streak of lightning blasted into the towering oak. Kelsie shrieked, her pinched face angled toward the tree falling right at them both.

The hand on Rebecca's shoulder shoved. She surged forward and tackled Kelsie, knocking them both clear of the heavy trunk seconds before it bashed into the ground.

Someone screamed.

Everything went black.

TWENTY

A voice called her name. "Rebecca!"

She opened her eyes. She was sprawled on her stomach next to a tumble of dark, quivering branches. A roar filled her ears. She lifted her head and struck a ceiling of wet leaves. To her right lay a black, hulking shape.

The tree. The trunk had missed her.

Where was Kelsie?

Rebecca pushed to her knees, ignoring the shooting pain in her arms and keeping her head tucked low under the branches. A few feet away, Kelsie was flat on her back, eyes closed. Rebecca reached out and touched her ankle. It felt cold.

"Are you guys okay?" Nick's voice was desperate.

Kelsie gave a strangled groan. Rebecca sagged with relief. "I think so."

Kelsie's eyes fluttered. "She . . . where?"

"Hold on, let me try to move this branch," Nick said. Then the leaves were up and away and a burning smell filled Rebecca's nose. Gray smoke rose from the smoldering tree stump. Her body felt numb with shock. She and Kelsie could've been struck by lightning. Or crushed by the tree.

But Sara had saved them. Somehow, she'd known what was coming and pushed Rebecca into Kelsie and out of danger. The two girls locked eyes, and a spark of understanding flew between them. They were lucky to be alive.

Through her tears, Rebecca noticed the sky growing lighter.

———

Kelsie's legs wobbled too much for her to walk on her own, so Nick and Rebecca helped her back to the Schmidt farmhouse. The lightning that had struck the tree had been the last gasp of the storm—the rain and wind cleared out by the time they got there. They each texted their parents, telling them they'd been caught in the storm but were safe. In the short time they waited at the Schmidts', Rebecca, Nick, and Kelsie didn't talk. When

Mom arrived, she hugged Rebecca tightly. The tornado sirens had gone off at the fairgrounds, forcing everyone to shelter in a concrete exhibition hall.

"I was so worried about you, sweetie," she said.

Back at Uncle Jon's, Rebecca crawled into bed early. She slept hard through the night without dreaming at all.

When Rebecca woke in the morning, the clock didn't make sense at first. No way could it be ten thirty. As she threw off the covers, pain shot through her body. She fell back onto the bed. Why was she sore?

The memories came flooding back. Sara's gravestone. The root cellar. The ghost. The lightning.

The falling tree that had almost crushed her and Kelsie.

Rebecca shuddered. Lying in her cozy bed with sunlight streaming through the curtains, her memories of the day before seemed like scenes from a scary movie she'd watched, not like real life. But her aching muscles proved it had happened.

She carefully got out of bed, went to her dresser, and opened the top drawer. Sara's locket nestled between her T-shirts. Rebecca pushed the clasp and it sprung open, revealing two black-and-white photos inside. The one on the left was a miniature version of Clara's baby picture, exactly like the one she'd found in the trunk. The photo on the right appeared to be the same baby posed in a different position. But now Rebecca knew it wasn't the same baby. It was Sara. The fact that they'd been identical twins made the whole story even more painful. She closed the locket and carefully put it back in the drawer.

As she dressed, Rebecca went over what she'd learned. A lot of mysteries had been solved, but new ones had come to the surface. What had happened to Sara in the summer of 1900? And what had Sara meant when she said "Not again"?

Someone knocked on the door.

"Come in," Rebecca said.

Mom poked her head into the room. "Hey. You were so tired last night, I let you sleep in. I've got to run some errands, but I have a minute to cook you some scrambled eggs, if you want."

"Sure. Where is everyone else?"

"Sylvie and Jon took Justin to her doctor's appointment, so he can hear the baby's heartbeat."

"That's cool." As Mom retreated into the hall, Rebecca stopped her. "Hold on."

Mom reappeared, smiling. "Yes, Co-Cap?"

"Um." Rebecca wrapped one of her curls around a finger, struggling to figure out what to say. After all she'd faced in the last twenty-four hours, she knew how brave she could be, but pushing this topic with her mom took a different kind of strength. She had to do it, though. "Are you positive Dad never told you he'd been into ghosts when he was a kid?"

Mom's smile wavered. "Oh." She pressed her lips together for a second, then stepped into the room. "I haven't been completely honest with you, honey."

Rebecca's stomach clenched. "What are you talking about?"

"I probably ought to tell you," Mom said softly, almost to herself. She pulled the rocking chair closer to the bed and sank into it, clasping her hands in her lap. "Sit, please."

Rebecca anxiously lowered herself onto the bed.

"I did know about your dad's fascination with ghosts," Mom said.

"You did?" Rebecca went still.

"Yes." Mom twisted her hands. "He even told me he thought he'd sensed one here at the farm when he was young."

"Mom, are you serious?" Everything in the room seemed to tilt. Rebecca clutched the edge of the mattress beneath her.

"Let me finish, please." Mom's eyes glistened. "Your dad and I always joked that whoever died first, me or him, their spirit would come back and make contact with the other. To let them know they were okay. But . . . he never came back. Ever. And I waited and pleaded and . . ." Her tears spilled, and she wiped her cheeks. "So, when you started with all the ghost stuff a few years ago, I had to nip it in the bud, before you were disappointed, too. Because someday you would've wanted to see him. And it was never going to happen. Ghost stories are just stories, not reality."

A noise escaped Rebecca's lips, half laugh, half sob.

Mom placed her hand on Rebecca's arm and continued. "Then last night I had a bad dream. I've never told anyone this, but the last few years I've had this odd thing happen when I have a nightmare." Her gaze drifted to the window. "At the scariest point, I feel a hand touching my shoulder, like someone's telling me 'Everything is fine, it's only a dream.'"

Rebecca's eyes widened. "That happens to me, too!"

"It does?" Mom's focus snapped to Rebecca. "While you're dreaming?"

"Yes! Then I can wake myself up, and I'm not scared anymore."

Mom blinked away her tears. "That makes this even more special. Last night I had a terrible nightmare. About a storm. Probably because of the tornado warning yesterday. Anyway, for some reason, in the dream, when I felt the pressure on my shoulder, I turned around. I've never done that before, I've always just woken up. But last night I was able to see who was behind me."

"And?" Rebecca gripped Mom's hand.

"It was your dad."

Rebecca gasped. "Really?"

"Yes, he was standing there, touching my shoulder. Smiling his beautiful smile at me. And then I woke up." Mom leaned closer. "And I realized something important. His love has been with me the whole time, even if he hasn't. I don't need to see his ghost to know that."

"Mom, I always thought it was you touching my shoulder in those dreams." Rebecca's own eyes brimmed. "Do you think . . . ?"

"Oh, Co-Cap, yes." Mom gently wiped the tears spilling on Rebecca's cheeks. "Deep down your heart knows that your dad's love is always with you, too."

They hugged for a long moment.

Finally, Mom pulled away and brushed a stray curl away from Rebecca's forehead. "For the record, I still don't believe in ghosts. But love doesn't go away. It lives on. That I do believe. And I'm sorry, I know I sometimes push you away when you want to talk about your dad. That's wrong of me. I see you soak up the stories Jon tells you about him and I realize you need more than one day a year to really talk about him. I thought I was doing the right thing, not letting you dwell, but—"

"It's okay, Mom." Rebecca cleared her throat. "Now, it's my turn to tell you something."

The doorbell chimed.

Mom rose from the chair. "Hold that thought, Co-Cap."

TWENTY-ONE

Rebecca followed Mom down the stairs, not wanting to be apart from her yet. Her mind swirled with pictures and thoughts. Dad's love was still real. It wasn't gone or trapped in the past; it stayed with her always. A warm glow spread through her.

Mom opened the front door. Kelsie was pacing on the porch, a backpack slung over her shoulders.

"What a nice surprise!" Mom said.

Rebecca wasn't so sure. She braced herself for Kelsie's usual nasty attitude.

"Hi, Ms. Graff. Hi, Rebecca." Kelsie's mouth turned up slightly at the corners. Rebecca had never seen her smile. As faint as it was, the smile transformed her entire face, making her seem much younger.

Mom checked her watch. "You know, I have a

conference call with my principal this afternoon, and I need to get my errands done before that. Co-Cap, can you grab breakfast on your own? We can have lunch together later. And talk more."

"Sure. I'm not really hungry now, anyway," Rebecca said.

Mom kissed her cheek and dashed upstairs. Rebecca joined Kelsie on the porch and closed the door behind her. "How are you feeling?" she asked.

"Fine, actually." Surprisingly, even after yesterday's near miss with the tree, Kelsie looked much better than she had lately. The dark circles beneath her eyes had faded. She rummaged around inside the backpack. "Here. This belongs to you." She thrust a dented, dirty cookie tin at Rebecca.

"Is this . . . is this the treasure box?" Rebecca could hardly believe she was finally holding it in her hands.

"Yes." Though the weather had cooled off a ton after the storm, Kelsie's forehead glistened with sweat. She didn't meet Rebecca's eyes. "It's all there, exactly like I found it. Well, except for the one locket. You already have that."

Rebecca balanced the tin on the porch railing, took a deep breath, and pried off its lid.

A few small items rested inside—an arrowhead, a tarnished silver thimble, two heart-shaped stones, a small book. There was a dingy handkerchief with a name embroidered in pale-blue thread: Sara Evangeline. A second handkerchief nestled in a corner, knotted into a bundle. Kelsie pointed at it.

"Open that up."

Rebecca carefully untied the handkerchief and found a heart-shaped locket on a dull gold chain, the exact match of the one in her dresser drawer. Exact except for the order of the initials. Her fingertips grazed the letters engraved on the surface, a *C* on the left and an *S* on the right. She sprang the clasp. The photos inside were identical to those in the other locket.

"Wow." Rebecca didn't know what else to say.

"Now check inside the cover of the book."

Rebecca lifted the book, titled *Poems for a Summer Day*. The name *Sara Evangeline Foxx* flowed across the first page in a fancy cursive script.

"See?" Kelsie said, a trace of her usual sass in her voice. "The name there is Sara *Foxx*. Not Graff. How was I supposed to know she was related to you?"

"Fair." Mom's car backed down the driveway. Rebecca waved, and Mom beeped her horn.

"I should go," Kelsie said, scratching at the rash on her arm.

"Wait," Rebecca said. "Is that from poison ivy?"

"Yeah." Kelsie lifted her arm glumly. "I should've known

digging that box out would be trouble. I saw the poison ivy around it, but I couldn't help myself."

"Tell me again how you found it?"

Kelsie sagged against the porch railing. "It's so boring here. My dad and my grandpa are always busy." Her voice grew soft. "I'd go exploring on my own. Sometimes I even sneaked out with a flashlight at night, just to make it more exciting. The night I found the box, I was by the creek, and it started pouring. All the rain, like, washed away some dirt, and I saw the corner of the box sticking out."

"Hold up." Rebecca had a hunch. "Do you remember what night it was?"

"Yes. Because that's the night I started having nightmares and not being able to sleep."

Rebecca gaped at her. "What kind of nightmares?"

"I don't know. There was always lightning and thunder and screaming." Kelsie shuddered. "The first one happened the night before the barbecue here."

Whoa. Rebecca's hunch was right. That was the night she'd had to close her window because of the rain and spotted a light bobbing around the Schmidt farm. It had been Kelsie out exploring with her flashlight. She thought back. And hadn't her bad dreams begun that night, too? "You didn't tell anyone you found the box?"

"No, why would I? It was my secret. All mine." Kelsie lifted her chin defiantly.

Rebecca couldn't blame her. She hadn't told her own family about what she'd discovered lately, either. It was always hard to know how adults would react to stuff. "Were you really going to sell it?"

Kelsie ducked her head. "I thought I could get some good money for it and buy a bus ticket to L.A. I miss my mom so much, and my dad doesn't want me to go right now. I thought maybe I could talk her into coming back to us."

"Oh." Rebecca really didn't know what to say to that. She touched Kelsie's elbow. "Thank you for bringing this to me. Really."

"What else was I supposed to do?" Kelsie hugged her backpack to her chest. "I saw that ghost. I was so scared. But she pushed us out of the way of that tree. She saved our lives. If she wants the locket back, fine. I wasn't sure if I should bury it again or what. So I thought I should give it to you."

A soft breeze swirled around the porch. Rebecca's phone buzzed in her pocket. She took it out. There was a text from Nick.

Can I come over?

She texted back a thumbs-up. "Nick's on his way over."

"Oh. I gotta go." Kelsie slung her backpack across her shoulder and practically ran down the steps.

"You don't have to," Rebecca called, surprised. "You can stay."

"No. I'm not really up for seeing Nick right now. I'm outta here." Kelsie wheeled her bike to the driveway and hopped on. "See you around."

It made sense that Kelsie might be embarrassed to face Nick. Rebecca settled in one of the wicker chairs and waited. He made it to the house in record time. Like Kelsie, he had a backpack. As he came up the porch steps, he pulled out a slightly crushed bouquet of wildflowers.

"Um, these are for you," he said, awkwardly pushing the purple-and-white bunch at Rebecca. "Hope you're not allergic to any of them."

"Me too." No one had ever given Rebecca flowers before. She glanced at him shyly. "Thanks. Come on, I'll put them in water."

"Is anyone here?" Nick asked as they went inside.

Rebecca noticed Jade slinking alongside him, making herself at home. "No."

"Okay, then, how are you?"

"Not bad, considering." Rebecca grabbed a vase from the kitchen windowsill and turned on the tap water. "But I can't believe it all happened."

"Me neither." Nick's eyes drooped as if he hadn't slept much. "That ghost was real. What . . . What *was* all that?"

Rebecca slid the flowers into the vase. "I'm still trying to figure it all out."

She explained everything that had happened before she'd run into him at Meadow Winds during the storm— how she'd used Clara's picture to find where the willow had stood, discovered the gravestone, and guessed that Kelsie had Sara's locket. Nick listened without interrupting.

"So Sara died when she was twelve. But I don't know how," Rebecca said, finishing her story.

Nick unzipped his backpack and retrieved his phone. "Let's look it up on the internet."

"Wait," Rebecca said. "Let's use a computer."

As she ushered him outside and to the barn, Jade scampered along.

"I guess the cat is curious, too," Nick said.

Rebecca couldn't laugh at his joke. Her stomach knotted nervously. She might finally be on the brink of figuring out the mystery of the ghost.

She sat at Mom's desk, logged in, then entered Sara's full name.

A newspaper article from 1900 popped onto the screen.

LOCAL GIRL KILLED BY LIGHTNING STRIKE

"Oh, no," Rebecca whispered. Her throat closed. Nick read over her shoulder.

> Twelve-year-old Sara Foxx of County Road M was struck and killed by lightning Saturday night, July 28, on her family's farm. Sara is survived by her father, William Foxx, a prominent local farmer, and her twin sister, Clara. She was preceded in death by her mother, Eleanor Reimers Foxx. Funeral services are pending.

Rebecca's eyes followed a line of dust motes twirling in a beam of sunlight coming through the window. She tried to imagine the horror of having someone you love struck by lightning. Your identical twin, no less.

"Yesterday was July 28," Nick said quietly.

Rebecca slumped in the chair. "So that's what Sara meant when she said, 'Not again'—she was talking about the storm. She *did* know Kelsie was in danger."

"Wow. And she saved you guys."

"The book I'm reading—the ghost story book—said ghosts sometimes appear as omens, when conditions are right, to warn people. Like they know when history is going to repeat itself."

"That is wild," Nick said. "I don't get one thing, though. How come there was nothing about Sara in the trunk or the diary? And didn't your uncle tell you Clara was an only child? It's like she was totally forgotten."

Jade yowled from the main room. A sudden chill nipped the air, and something smacked the floor behind them. Rebecca and Nick turned. A battered paper copy of *The Old Farmer's Almanac 1955* had tumbled from the bookshelf. Jade shot over to it, hissing. The chill receded.

"Did you feel that?" Rebecca said.

Nick's eyebrows had shot up as far as they could go. "I think you're supposed to look in that book."

Rebecca scooped it off the floor, thinking back. "You know what? When I saw the ghost that night in the barn, I totally heard something fall in here. And it came at me across the floor . . ." She shuddered, remembering. "Maybe this is what it was trying to show me."

She opened the cover. The table of contents listed stuff like monthly weather predictions, lunar cycles, even recipes. What did any of that have to do with the ghost? Unless . . . Rebecca riffled through the pages and triumphantly pulled out a cream-colored envelope.

"Seriously?" Nick rolled his eyes. "What is it with your family hiding stuff in books?"

"It must be genetic." Rebecca couldn't help giggling.

Even she sometimes used the torn picture of Clara as a bookmark in *Heart-Stopping Heartland Hauntings*.

The envelope was only partially addressed to a Mrs. Heinrich Graff on Santa Ana Street and wasn't sealed. As Rebecca removed a piece of stationery, her smile dissolved. "It's a letter from Clara."

She read out loud.

March 4, 1955
Dear Aunt Gertrude,

"Oh." Rebecca exhaled with a mix of amazement and relief. "Gertrude was her aunt, not her stepmom."

"Huh?" Nick said.

"I'll tell you later."

She read on.

I hope this letter finds you well. Maybe someday I can visit you in California, and we can eat oranges in the sunshine and talk about the old days. Time moves so quickly and family is important.

I'm writing to let you know I've come to a decision. I've been reflecting about life and death—perhaps because of my advancing age, perhaps because my grandson Sam and his wife are expecting a baby, my first great-grandchild. Regardless, it is time. I am going to tell my family about Sara.

I know you may not approve. After all, you and Uncle Heinrich came to Iowa in part to help Father and me move on. I can hear you now—"If you focus on the future, Clara, the past can't hurt you." I understand your intentions were good and I'm not blaming you for anything. And you did help me get over the memory of Sara's scream that awful night. But I need you to understand why I believe it was wrong of me to pretend Sara never existed.

I was devastated when she passed. We'd always been two parts of the same whole. I've never told anyone this, but she came to me in a dream six months after her death. She told me not to mourn, to go on with my life, and that she was happy with Mother in heaven. Father said the same. He built the new house for us and never spoke of Sara again.

But I was so young. I was confused and sad and angry. I felt abandoned by my twin and hurt that she was fine without me. Because I was not fine without her.

So to punish her, to please Father, and to cut myself off from my pain, I forced myself to forget. I went on with my life. And Sara stayed tucked away inside my heart.

Lately, though, she has come back to me in my dreams. I don't know why, but I think perhaps she's always been watching over me, probably sad to have been forgotten.

I'm going to dig up the treasure box Sara and I shared in our childhood. I buried it near her grave when we moved to the new house. In it are two lockets. I believe now that it was wrong to deny this part of myself, and I want to rectify my mistake. All feelings, whether good or bad, are part of being human. I intend to honor Sara and wear my locket again. And, if this new baby is a girl, I will give her Sara's.

I'm excited to share part of my own generation with the new generation. I'd love to have your blessing.

Please write when you can.

Your loving niece, Clara

Rebecca let her hand holding the letter drop to the desk. An idea nudged her. Clara had buried all thoughts of her twin after Sara had died. She herself had never gone that far—but until lately hadn't she always pushed away her sadness about Dad? If Clara was right, that only caused more problems.

"I don't get it," Nick said, breaking into the silence. "No one ever found this?"

"I guess not. Look at the date." Rebecca showed Nick the paper. "Old Mr. Schmidt said Clara died suddenly right before this baby was born. I think she was writing about my dad's dad, Andrew, who would've been her great-grandson. And maybe she stuck it in here before she could mail it and then . . . she died? No one was expecting that, and then the baby came, and who knows? The book got put away and forgotten."

"Man." Nick's forehead wrinkled with concern.

Rebecca rubbed her arms to get rid of the lingering coldness. She'd always believed life was easier for grown-ups. But Clara obviously hadn't figured stuff out until she was an old lady.

Footsteps thudded in the barn. "Rebecca?" Mom was out of breath.

"In here," Rebecca called.

Mom arrived in the doorway. "Sylvie is at the hospital! The baby's coming!"

TWENTY-TWO

Rebecca cut away the last prickly branch, tossed it in the trash bag, and peeled off her gardening gloves.

"Done," she said to Nick. "Now we can put this back where it belongs."

The two stood on the dusty bank by the creek. July's torrential rains had dried up and given way to August's sunny, oven-like heat. Late-summer cicadas blasted their buzz-saw song from the wild coneflowers and black-eyed Susans decorating the water's edge. It was time to rebury the treasure box where Clara had placed it so many years ago.

For a moment Rebecca tipped her face to the sun, soaking in its warmth. So much had happened in the past few weeks.

Most important, of course, Olivia Anne Graff had

been born. Even though she'd arrived several weeks early, both she and Aunt Sylvie were healthy and thriving. Uncle Jon was totally gaga over his daughter, and Justin danced around yelling "I'm a big bro!" constantly. Olivia's tiny fingers, her delicate eyebrows, her velvety sheen of blond hair fascinated Rebecca. And, to her delight, Olivia seemed to have the family eyes.

It astonished her how much work it took to care for one tiny human. Since Olivia had come home, Rebecca had been so busy watching Justin and helping around the house, she hadn't had much time to think about Clara and Sara. The whole family was in constant, happy chaos. Her and Mom's day of fun together had been postponed because of Olivia's arrival, but Rebecca didn't mind. All their bickering and disagreements had evaporated, and their team was solid again. She knew they'd have ups and downs in the future, but somehow everything that had happened this summer had cemented a new bond between them.

The day Olivia and Aunt Sylvie were scheduled to come home from the hospital, Rebecca had wandered onto the front porch with her orange juice and found an envelope taped to the door. Her name was written in hot-pink marker across the front. She ripped it open and fished out a note.

Dear Rebecca,

Sorry about everything. My dad
is letting me go visit my mom
for a while. I'm leaving today.
You'll probably be gone by the
time I get back. Good luck with
Nick.

Kelsie

Rebecca had cringed. "Good luck with Nick"—geez, was it that obvious?

Sara's ghost hadn't appeared since the night of the big storm.

Jenna was home from camp, and she and Rebecca had been texting and talking on the phone nonstop. Of course, Rebecca had forgiven her for the lame letters from camp and gotten her up to speed on everything that had happened. They planned an epic sleepover for the first night Rebecca got home, so Jenna could hear every single detail in person, from beginning to end.

"You need to write your own ghost story," Jenna kept saying.

Since Olivia had been born, Rebecca had gone to watch two of Nick's baseball games, but this afternoon was the first chance she'd had to really talk with him. A small party for the baby was taking place at Uncle Jon and Aunt Sylvie's. During the picnic lunch earlier, Rebecca and Nick had eaten alone on a blanket under the backyard maple.

First she showed him the new discovery she'd made. Uncle Jon had relented and allowed her to go up in the attic on her own after he'd checked to make sure nothing could topple over on her. She'd gone through the trunk again and found something she'd missed before. Part of a torn photo was stuck to the back of a Sears catalog—the other half of the photo she'd found at Meadow Winds. She'd carefully taped the two halves together to make a whole.

"Wow," Nick said, looking at the restored photo.

The right side of the picture, the part Rebecca had discovered in the attic, showed the trunk of the willow tree and a second girl. This girl had the same fluffy, light hair as her sister standing next to her, but her face wasn't blurred. And she definitely had the family eyes. The two girls were identical, down to the dresses they wore.

On the back, the two halves together revealed the full message.

Clara
And
Sara
May 1900

The picture had been taken two months before Sara's death.

Nick studied the photo, then burst out laughing. Rebecca knew exactly why. In the bottom right corner, peering around the base of the willow, was a black, one-eyed cat.

"Are you kidding me?" he said. "Does this mean Jade is a ghost?"

"Well, I haven't seen her for a while. It's like she's disappeared." Rebecca grinned. "But I did pet her before, and she sure felt real. Who knows, maybe she's a descendant of Sara and Clara's cat?"

"Or . . ." Nick waggled his finger at her. "Maybe that was her first life. And this is her ninth."

"Ha! True!"

Rebecca also described the nightmares she'd had all summer and how they'd grown scarier and more detailed. "They started the night Kelsie says she found the treasure box."

"Sara's ghost must've known right away the locket had been messed with," Nick said through a mouthful of ham sandwich.

"Right," said Rebecca, picking up her cup of lemonade. "And that disturbed her peace, you know? My dad's list described Sara's ghost as sad and just kinda hanging around. Maybe she was watching over the family and hoping to be remembered. But then two things happened. One, Kelsie took the locket. And, two, the stormy weather was the same as the summer she died. So she was on a mission to get the locket back and to stop history from repeating itself. My ghost book says some spirits, like, know when something bad is about to happen. Especially if it happened to them when they were alive."

She swirled her cup in a circle, watching the liquid slosh against the sides, picturing the horrible thunderstorm in her mind.

Nick wiped some crumbs off his chin. "Clara's letter said Sara talked to her at least once in a dream. So that was one of her ways of communicating. She used dreams to warn you—and Kelsie, I guess—about the storm. And your dreams got scarier as she got stronger and more worried. I've read about some other cases like this."

"Seriously?" Rebecca socked him in the arm. "Two weeks ago you were a complete doubter and now you're a paranormal scientist?"

Nick flushed and plucked at the picnic blanket. "Yeah, so? I've been doing a little research online." He laughed and threw his sandwich crust at Rebecca. "Okay, busted. But it all makes total sense." He grinned, dimple on display. She grinned right back, and her insides went squishy. She had to look away.

Her gaze traveled across the yard to Mom and Mark. They sat at opposite ends of the picnic table, Mom hanging with Dr. Li and Mark next to Uncle Jon. As far as Rebecca knew, the two of them hadn't gone out since Olivia had been born. Maybe their romance really wasn't serious. Rebecca couldn't figure it out. But Mom had definitely been concentrating more on family the last two weeks. She and Uncle Jon said they had a whole amazing plan figured out to celebrate Dad's birthday. Rebecca couldn't wait.

Mom would probably go on more dates in the future. Rebecca figured she could accept that. Things would work out.

"What about the curse stuff?" Nick asked.

"Yeah, I've been thinking about that. I think that was just Clara being dramatic. Who would blame her?"

"Except for the fact that Kelsie had bad dreams and couldn't sleep after she stole the treasure box," Nick said. "And obviously got poison ivy."

"You're right. Maybe we'll never know." Rebecca grabbed her backpack with the tin inside. "Let's go. We'd better do this while we have the chance." The two of them had left the party and sneaked off to the creek.

Now, admiring the sparkling water and loving the sun's delicious warmth on her skin, Rebecca could hardly believe July had happened. Or that this beautiful place had been the site of so much turmoil. Meadow Winds had been demolished. The blackened tree stump had been bulldozed away. She and Kelsie had almost been killed here. Clara had grieved here. Sara had died here.

Nick used a shovel as a lever to pop up the flat stone marked with the hearts, uncovering the hole where the box had been buried. "Ready?"

Rebecca ran her hands over the tin container. To her surprise tears stung her eyes. It would be hard to let the box go, to say goodbye to this small part of Clara and Sara. She hoped with all her heart that putting it back where it belonged would bring peace to Sara's spirit.

The sun dipped behind a cloud. The cicada drone cut off abruptly, replaced by a low buzz. Time slowed. A shadow slid up from the depths of the creek.

Sara.

Rebecca gasped. Nick froze, shovel poised in the air. Sara's face wavered beneath the surface of the water. This time her hair floated gently around her head, and her mouth didn't gape but curved into a sweet smile. Her hand appeared at her throat, then pointed at Rebecca.

"The locket?" Rebecca whispered. "Yes, we're going to put it back."

Sara shook her head, touched her throat again, and pointed at Rebecca.

"I don't . . . what do you mean?" Rebecca said.

"Rebecca," Nick said. "She wants you to keep her locket."

"What?"

Sara nodded. Rebecca swayed on her feet, overwhelmed. A breeze ruffled the leaves in the woods. Sara smiled gently—and melted away.

Immediately the cicadas resumed screeching, and bright sunshine burst from behind the cloud. Rebecca blinked in the light.

"That's . . ." Nick shook his head. "Wow. Of course you should keep the locket. It's only right."

We did it, Dad, Rebecca thought.

His "Signs of the Ghost" had boosted her, reassured her that the spooky things she experienced were truly happening. Knowing he'd believed in the ghost and wanted to find out what it wanted had pushed her to solve the mystery. And helped Sara find peace.

Her cell phone beeped and vibrated in her pocket. She plucked it out and read the text from her mom: *Time for presents!*

At the party everyone gathered around the picnic table to watch Sylvie open gifts. Rebecca stayed to one side of the crowd, hiding her present for Olivia behind her back. The adults oohed and aahed over the adorable little baby clothes and trinkets while the guest of honor slept peacefully in Uncle Jon's arms.

Mom showed up next to Rebecca and gave her a gentle nudge. "What's that present you have there?" she whispered.

Rebecca put a finger to her lips. Mom looked at her curiously, but she said nothing. Rebecca caught Nick's eye across the crowd. He winked. She blushed.

Aunt Sylvie rose from her chair, pastel-colored wrapping paper falling from her lap. "Thank you all for coming to welcome Olivia to the world! I—"

"Hold on," Rebecca interrupted. Everyone turned to look at her, and a tiny jab of jitters hit her. She forged ahead. "We're not done yet."

She had wrapped the perfect gift for Olivia—the christening gown and locket Clara had wanted to give her first great-grandchild. Tonight, she'd sit the family down and give them the full details of Sara's forgotten life and death, as well as the reasons why Clara never talked about her twin. She would tell them she'd found all of Clara's stuff, even the treasure box, the letter to Gertrude, and both sides of the torn photo, in the trunk in the attic. She would tell them she had stumbled across Sara's grave near the creek.

Sara's ghost, though, would stay secret between her, Nick, Kelsie, and Jenna.

The adults wouldn't understand.

"There's one more present." Rebecca held the box out to Aunt Sylvie with her right hand, while her left cradled Clara's locket. "And it comes with an amazing story."

ACKNOWLEDGMENTS

I have dreamed of becoming a published author since I was a little girl. In fifth grade I wrote—in pencil! in a flowered fabric–covered spiral notebook!—twelve chapters of a Nancy Drew–inspired novel that I never finished. About ten years ago I started writing again, and this book is the result.

Thank you to Alison Romig, my fantastic editor at Delacorte Press, for loving this story and expertly guiding me to make it better. It's been a joy to collaborate with you, and your professionalism and care have made this process so smooth. Everyone from Delacorte who worked on this book has been excellent—managing editor Tamar Schwartz, copy editors Liz Byer and Colleen Fellingham, publisher Beverly Horowitz, and publicist Lena Reilly. Thank you to cover designer Michelle Cunningham, interior designer Jen Valero, and cover artist Simon Padres—it's a dream come true to see my words and the world I pictured so beautifully rendered.

To my agent at BookStop Literary, Karyn Fischer: I'm

lucky to have you for a partner. Thank you for championing me and my writing. Your insight, intelligence, and dedication are unmatched.

I am grateful for my writer friends, especially Casey Lyall, Jenne Lehne, Sarah Rowlands, Lorien Lawrence, Brenda Drake, and the Pitch Wars class of 2015. Your friendship and counsel have meant the world to me. To Pamela Dell, writing coach extraordinaire, thank you for encouraging me, pushing me, and introducing me to the kidlit writers' world.

I have a wonderful family. Thank you to my dad, Tom, a fabulous storyteller. To my stepfather, Craig, who shares my love of history. To my stepmom, Kathy, who was with me on the Iowa bike ride many years ago when I came across the abandoned farmhouse that inspired this story. To my mom, Judy, who jump-started my love of reading by letting me into the attic one summer morning when I was seven, showing me her treasure trove of books from her childhood, and letting me pick one to read all by myself (for the record, I chose *The Haunted Bridge* by Carolyn Keene). And to my aunt Barb, who lived on a farm in Wisconsin when I was a kid, let me jump from the barn loft into piles of hay, and had a one-eyed black cat named Jade. Wish I could list everyone. Thank you all for your unwavering support.

My wonderful children, Will and Delaney, are a constant source of joy and inspiration. My husband believed in me and assisted me through this journey—Ted, this book wouldn't be what it is without you. I appreciate and love you all very much.

ABOUT THE AUTHOR

WENDY PARRIS grew up loving books and hoping—but failing—to see a ghost. After graduating from Northwestern University, she acted in small Chicago storefront theaters, performed improv comedy, and worked in public relations. When not thinking up spooky tales, she likes to kayak, bike, travel, and go to movies. She lives in Illinois with her family in an old house that is probably not haunted. *Field of Screams* is her debut novel.